9LiveZ

S
C

Space Cocaine is bad for you. Too much of a thing—especially *this* thing—and you might end up like the fellow on the cover of this issue.

If you must explore the wonders of *Space Cocaine*, remember that everything you experience while under the influence of *Space Cocaine* is a work of fiction. Names, characters, places, and incidents are the products of the author's imagination or are used in an absolutely fictitious manner. Any resemblance to actual events, locales, or persons—living or dead—is entirely coincidental.

This book was printed in the United States of America. It has been produced in association with Firebird Creative LLC. (Clackamas, OR).

There is a website where you can find others who equally enamored with *Space Cocaine*. The URL is what you expect:

spacecocaine.com

Always double-check your work. You probably forget something important . . .

9LiveZ

contents

Bumbleberries

Kate Ristau

"Tell me a story about a cat."
"Honey. It's late. Go to sleep."
"Story."
"No."
"Please?"
"Fine."

In a time that was and a time that wasn't, there lived a cat. She—

"He."

He had long whiskers, long claws, long fur, and was sassy as the day is long.

"I'm not sassy."
"I'm talking about the cat."
"I'm the cat."
"You're the boy, who is supposed to be listening to the story."
"I wish I was the cat."
"Do you?"
"It would be fun to be a cat."

"But then you wouldn't be my—"
"Oh, not for always. Just for, you know, a while."
"Just a little while?"
"Yeah."
"All right. Well . . ."

He loved milk and he loved muffins. He loved tea and he loved cookies. But most of all, he loved ADVENTURE. He always thought of it in big capital letters, like one of those fancy pages in a book. All big and swirly. He could smell it with his nose. It made his toes tingle. It smelled like ice cream. And bumbleberries.

"What are bumbleberries?"
"Shhh. Stop interrupting."
"I like blueberries."
"You've never even had a bumbleberry."
"Have you?"
"Yes."
"What do they taste like?"
"Blueberries."

And blueberries. All sweet and sugary. Well, one day he was walking down the forest path, thinking about dinner and dinosaurs and delicious D words, when—

"Oh no!"
"Grab it!"
"It's everywhere!"

"Get a towel."
"It's all over the nightstand."
"Honey, just calm down and get a towel."

D words like dumple. Deeple. Donagon. Dragon. Yes, dragon. That was a good D word.

"What did I miss?"
"Saying sorry."
"Sorry."
"For what?"
"Knocking over your water glass."
"Wipe it up, silly."
"There. Wipe. Swipe. Wiped out. Ha! Like a skater. Wipeout! All gone. Now, what'd I miss?"
"Dragons."
"Mom!"
"Shhh . . ."

He scraped his claws along the path, tiny bits of orange fur falling from his legs, sticking in the mud along the clawed-out tracks. Then he stuck his nose straight up into the—

"Do you have to do that?"
"It feels good. It's like I'm a cat."
"You're a boy."
"Rub my head."
"Fine. Just stop pushing it at me."

—air. He spun it around and around, up and down, and over and under, and through and in, and all those places in-between. He didn't trust his eyes. Not anymore. Five lives ago he'd been watching the stars and tripped over a cactus and landed straight on his—

"Ouch!"
"Sorry!"
"No scratching. Seriously."
"Sorry. Got it. Keep going."

—dumblebum. Now, he only trusted his nose. And if his nose knew anything, it was the smell of bumble—

"Blueberries."

Blueberries. Big juicy blueberries. Bright and blue bumbly bumbles.

"Mom? Will you look at my nails? They're getting so long. And sharp."

Bumbly blue berries. Soaked in the summer sun. Bumble-berries. Purple and violet and blue. All bumbling down.

"Mom?"
"What? Oh. Sorry. Sorry. I lost track. Where was I?"
"No. It's not that. It's just . . . um . . . do you smell something sweet?"

He turned his nose to the west and he saw it then, shadow and sun, coming down from the mountain, a trail of glorious fire lighting the sky.

"Why is it so bright outside?"

He grabbed his pack, slipping it over one furry shoulder. He was prepared. The dawn had broken. Bumbleberries were in the air. And if there was one thing he knew, it was the smell of ADVENTURE.

Moksha

Remy Nakamura

Nine.

You will die today. You have lived a good life, praise Little Cat, the best a wandering Feline could hope for. You killed your enemies by tooth, claw, and sharpened stone and gulped down the steaming intestines of your rivals, you broke the bones of each with a satisfying crunch. Following a repeated vision, you led your band out of the Endless Desert into this sharp valley full of fat marmots and docile rabbits.

You drove out humans, those towering furless apes, ugly like naked mole-rats. They were intelligent, but not as cunning as you and your kin. You trapped them in their caves with smoke and fire, and slew the screaming survivors with your slinging fangs of flint.

On this high crag, your attendants attend more to their nerves than to you, perhaps rightfully so. In the dark before dawn, death can pounce as dire wolves from below or descend as great predatory birds from above. In spite of their fear, these kits are loyal and refuse to leave you. You growl at them to stop wringing their raccoon-like paws and to attend to your final scritches.

In the dim light, the valley you called home is visible below, but on this night, your last night, you want the heavens to keep you company. Your secret guide was the bright star at the tip of Little Cat's tail. As long as you kept it behind you, you knew you could find your tribe a new home, one not parched by the sun, one in which the game was more fat than bones. In the sky are greater queens and matriarchs, leopards and sabretooths, even a cave bear, but it was Little Cat that saved you.

The growing dawn thins your attendants' pupils to sharp incisions. One golden ray catches like a claw on a puffy white flower: Lion's Tooth, growing improbably from a lichenous crack. It is in full seed, waiting to ride the wind, and it glows, an aspirational sun. How can anything so simple, so inconsequential, be so beautiful?

It explodes in the sliver of time before the great eagle takes you up into the sky.

Eight.

You are in hell. Or you may as well be, especially in the growing desert's brutal summers. The night is no respite, because your calling is to spend it in front of the glowing, pulsating heat of your family's kiln. You long for the coolness of the snow-capped mountains in the distance, but you are a glassblower, as was your mother, your grandfather, and their parents before them.

In desperation some years ago, you shaved your long fur off. The humiliation and rejection you suffered burned more painfully than a firebrand on a forepaw.

What does provide respite is your newfound purpose. You have a client who admires your dexterity and skill. You, in turn, admire the shine of his silver fur and the shine in his eyes, one icy blue, the other amber gold. Just the thought of him makes you arch your long back. You pour all your skill, all your craft into a gift for him, a gift to win his heart.

You still make the ornate cream saucers and dinner plates commissioned by the city-state's nobility, but each night you return to your masterwork. It is something that haunts your dreams: a single dandelion, trapped in a ray of light, ready to burst. You stretched a long delicate stem and shaped leaves that look cut from raw emeralds. On its diamond-like head, dozens of needle seeds made from silver strands of hair-thin glass.

The project has taken you nearly a year. Some nights you can only place, by tweezer or claw, a single careful filament. You fret that in the meantime someone else will capture his heart, but this is how you will declare your love, and art cannot be hurried.

The universe, sadly, knows nothing of love, or art. The earthquake hits—the most powerful to strike the Persian capital in centuries of recorded history—and crushes you, your love, your unfinished masterpiece, and all the hopes and futures connected to it.

Glitch.

A nightmare. You are in a field of yellow dandelions. You tower above them in a flame-repellent suit. Under it you know you are not a cat. You wear a flamethrower.

Every night you dream feline dreams.

But not always.

For endless cycles, you floated in oceans of water and oceans of space as ever-evolving cephalopods.

Faunal morphologies fall in and out of fashion. Canine. Ursine. Corvidae. Even capybaras. Sentient jellies.

A life lived as bioflesh, however long ago, is the grain of grit, the kernel around which quadrillions of quantum algorithmic synapses form new identities. Embodied histories provide metaphors and emotional hooks to which cling simulated life. They form the scaffolding, provide the structural support to fight entropy, to fight suicide, and worst of all, to fight boredom.

But no matter how many eons pass, you always cover, hide, reject your human origins. You, as collective humanity, doomed your home. You didn't know how priceless that pearl was, but you threw it away. This is the unforgivable sin that cast you into outer darkness.

You wish you could erase this part of your past.

You flood the field of yellow flowers with napalm. Because this is what humans do. Flames spread across the field, the continent, the surface of the planet. Oily smoke fills the atmosphere, penetrates your facemask, acrid petrol stabbing your sinuses. Shame for the sins of your ancestors consumes you from within, and white-hot flame blackens you from without.

You welcome what oblivion you can find.

Six.

Today's object of meditation is a weed, a dandelion. You smack your dry mouth. This lone flower emerged from a crack in the crumbling arch that serves as the entrance to the courtyard. You used to think of the precarious stone blocks as a good reminder of the transience of life, but the monks in your abbey have more immediate concerns. Storerooms and stomachs are empty, and this week there are reports of pillaging Calicos. Although it is a warm spring day, the air tastes like smoke. Any added reminders of mortality are redundant.

The flower. You struggle to focus these days. The plant is tenacious, growing upside down. Its white sphere contains the promise and hope of future fields of yellow flowers. How did one seed land on this inhospitable crack, and how did the sprout find the soil it needed to grow into a mature dandelion?

In the hand-carved tunnels below, your novices hide and seal away the true treasure of this abbey: an illustrated encyclopedia of your civilization, scribed by ink and foreclaw onto thousands of vellum scrolls. You hope that your life's work will survive. You hope that a few of your followers will flee and sire kittens.

A single seed tears away from the dandelion, hovering for a moment.

Satori.

Your dreams, of eagles in the sun, of hot forges, these are of past lives. You suppress every impulse to leap up and write down this insight, to share this enlightenment with your spiritual children, but it is a revelation for you and for you alone.

Too many questions remain.

Is your life simply the dream of your next incarnation? What container holds all the dreams of your lives? Does everyone else dream, too?

You are disappointed to discover that Enlightenment is just the first step of the journey, and not its end.

The raiding party announces their arrival with hissing and growling. You prepare to parlay, to buy your monks more time. Instead, you hear the twang of claws releasing multiple bowstrings, like the strum of a strange instrument. The dandelion explodes.

Five.

```
Systems online.
Loading...
Loading...
Loading...
Abort, Retry, Ignore?
> Ignore
```

Four point four seven eight.

You knew from the get-go that Mars would kill you. You only left home when you realized that odds were that Earth would kill you faster. Thanks, Algorithmic Actuaries, Inc.! And now you're here in this rusty dusty paradise, carving out the crust with your crew.

As dangerous as Mars is, one of the great benefits of being an Amazelon Mars Corp. employee is that you have a backup! Making a copy of all that stuff in your head is actually pretty cheap, but cloning a body and restoring from backup is expensive, so it totally makes sense that you get a year added to your contract every time they have to reboot you.

Some of your crew members are worried about the legal claws that let Management make tiny edits to your persona, but that's mostly to fix radiation damage, right? So that's fine by you. AMC is a great place to work—you might even apply for a non-indentured position in a couple of days when your employment term is up. Mars sure ain't gonna strip-mine itself!

"Fuckfuckf–" Caspian's broadcasted yowl bounces around in your ClearHelm before cutting off. You spot him in his pink suit (it may have been white at one time) bounding away on all fours in pure primal panic. Bad catnip trip?

Behind him, a single dandelion sprouts, grows tall, unfurls, seeds ready to catch the wind. It's huge—two meters tall, and kind of shiny. You've seen a lot of weird mechanical hybrid shit on this planet. This looks different, but same-ish enough that you wouldn't be surprised to find the AMC logo a thin layer of fine Mars powder.

Then seeds break off like darts and shoot towards each member of your crew. Some try to dodge, but these missiles track movement. Most of your friends stand like prey animals in shock. Through her helmet plastic, you see Dana's wide pupils mirror the dawning realization in your own. This isn't the first time. Or the last.

Three.

You step into the airlock. You were born just minutes ago, your persona the child of an Outer System Socialist virus and a Corporate Conglomerate Coalition wageslave, downloaded into a vacant cat-clone in an I-pod.

The rebel virus is surprisingly informative but also very impatient. What you want is caffeine, or a long nap on the sunward side of the habitat, but instead it gushes friendly heresies and sedition directly into your prefrontal cortex. It heads off the CCC propaganda, its subversive dialog running parallel to your wake-up protocols. You feel it deleting aspects of your persona that would otherwise keep your brain enslaved to the Corporations. The OSS virus voids fractal branches of Corporation-fed desires and pours new memories like mercury into these newly empty brain veins.

Your love for your corporate masters is suddenly excised and replaced with cool existential commitment to The People.

The replacement has unexpected, unintended effects. You are now a beret-wearing, chain-smoking cat in the La Résistance, except that Amazelon Prime are the Space Stasi and your Paris floats in the upper reaches of the Jovian atmosphere. Your claws reach for a cigarette pack that never existed. Putain de bordel de merde.

There are CCC Bot and AI factions that question the necessity of any flesh hybrids, but Adama Smith's invisible hand pervades even the cold reaches of interplanetary space, and felinus economicus was never a rational actor. If Reason prevailed, consumption would have stopped while Earth and Mars still had atmospheres.

In between the orbits of these ruined planets there spins a ring around the rosy sun, a lacey latticework of finely woven habitats. Whenever the CCC needed a new market to perpetuate their centuries-old pyramid scheme, they simply extruded a new extension to this world and populated it with consumer clones and wage slaves.

The Outer System is simply trying to outlast the Conglomeration. You see holo-wikis of what remains of Venus, Earth, Mars, atmospheres siphoned to fill the pipes, oceans to fill plumbing, planets dismantled for parts. The OSS has all the organics of Titan and the water of Europa and Enceladus. It has the gas giants. It's a long war, and the OSS can outlast the CCC. In the process, they're trying to save as many of you as possible. Because it's noble and all that.

As you emerge from your I-Pod, you realize that you're dead meat. As in, your meat will not survive. C'est la vie. But some copy of you can survive. Your life may be short, but it has purpose. You order a pack of Gauloises, a Zippo lighter, a pin-striped suit and fedora at the Xpress Xerox. All on credit of course—a benefit of being dead soon. You put on the freshly printed clothes and emerge into a shiny silicon corridor. Do the Felines passing by in the latest fashions look at you with suspicion? You play it cool. The cigarette is cheap, but calms your nerves.

The virus is surprisingly resourceful. Maybe virus isn't the right description. It has hijacked systems, printed copies of your backup into a form that can flee, fly through space to the safety of the Outer System. You run through a maze of similar-looking corridors, stopping only to pick up a package, ironically, at an Amazelon-FedUps locker.

In your bare paws, you cradle a spikey ball, a matte black dandelion head. You realize this moment is being repeated across the entire latticework, along a 1.2-billion-kilometer chain around the sun, personas waking into new bodies, picking up packages, and preparing to sacrifice a life barely begun in a desperate attempt for a future. There is at least one Charlize Theron cat-clone among them.

And so here you are, standing in an emergency airlock, all controls overridden with the help of Rebel Virus. The CCC authorities are aware that something is happening. They are lasering the door. You take one last drag, savor the moment, stamp the cigarette out. You are too cool to be hurried. Vive les Felines!

You open the airlock with the manual controls and are whooshed into space. In the moment before you lose consciousness, the ball splits into millions of pieces, brilliant for a moment, then disappearing into the dark.

Each seed has a full backup of your persona. Each will ride the solar winds quietly, invisibly, into the outer system, for decades, perhaps centuries. Upon reaching the orbits of the outer planets, they will turn on tiny beacons, hoping to be picked up by Outer System operatives, friends of the Rebel Virus, who will have the resources to put you into a new body, to send you on new missions.

You hope that one of you makes it.

Bonne chance.

Two.

This is it. The points of failure outweighed the redundancy built into the system. So much technology was new, barely tested. Interstellar propulsion. The shielding for the memory banks that stored your uploaded personas. Rapid vat growing of bodies from limited resources. The millions of potential issues with the download of digital personas into unfamiliar bodies.

And so, here you are: a desperate, last-ditch attempt to save Felinity rested on a dozen survivors of this interplanetary mission, and you are the only one who is sane. Half of the problems were caused by particle collisions to the quantum cubes storing your digital personas. Others came with the download process. No brainer, really. For centuries, hardware, software, wetware, when has anything worked without bugs on the first release?

Most—the worst, really—were on the surface of this barely habitable exoplanet, destroyed in a single act of sabotage, so it's just the skeleton crew left on the orbiting station: you; Toki, a naked ape with four arms, no legs, two tails; and Shu, the land octopus. They could grow anything, and they picked these ugly bodies? Toki is especially despicable to you. This mission was doomed before launch. Through the networked eyes, you see an unhinged Shu, raging, screaming hateful epithets at you while hammering at the emergency door with something in all eight of their arms. Toki is in his sleep pod crying into his hands.

It's time to scrap this mission. Delete and reboot. You fire a burst transmission back towards Earth, containing all status and error logs (petabytes of errors) and video feed from all the nanoeyes. You open a packet and watch the single dandelion seed, suddenly freed, jump and bury itself into the fur of your forepaw.

You've been fascinated with dandelions for many lives now. You dream dandelions. Their seeds float, embed everywhere. You wanted a delete option for this mission, and this seemed the most poetic. This mission is one seed. For Earth's survivors to survive, you need so many more.

You bioengineered this one to seek flesh. It's a dandelion in shape only. You'll be dead in minutes. When you let Toki in, new dandelions will burst from your fur and fire flechette seeds at them. They will find Shu, eventually, unless he seals that pod into his coffin. Either way, mission aborted. Time to reboot.

One.

You are born, again, mewling, on a kitten-sized ship plum-meting into the vast, black cosmos. You see, at once, in every direction, on every wavelength. On microwave, you grok the coldness of interstellar space, cosmic background radiation hovering just three ticks above absolute zero. On X-ray, a gaping gravitational maw at the center of the galaxy clutches and devours stars and systems, engulfing ancient elders and smothering stellar nurseries. The invisible omnipresence of dark matter weighs on you.

Your world is shaped like a dandelion seed: the cylindrical vessel contains and powers the simulation you live in, are a part of; a carbon-fiber stalk precedes the vessel, furling a parachute of filaments for furlongs, each the width of an atom, catching the wind of stellar radiation, riding dark energy waves and currents, channeling some of that power back to you. The sim is slowed down to conserve energy. Each thought, each synap-tic burst takes an hour or longer in Old Earth time.

You are not alone in this vessel. You are Legion, for you are many. You recall these words, spoken to a human God long gone, from a distant past, an accessory to planetcide. Every attempt to forget humanity is an attempt to execute this God for their crimes, to consign humanity to the prison of obliv-ion. But humanity continues its appeals process, and you cannot completely erase or forget.

You surface for moments like this only to realize that you are no different. How many trillions of seeds flood the galaxy? How many worlds and systems have you consumed just to make more copies of yourself, to defy entropy and push the boulder of life up the hill one more time?

Your companions in the multispectrum static nod sympathetically, ready for what comes next. They are bubbling in and out of the simulation, a froth of digital lives and deaths, churning through history and imagination, truths and lies. You dive back into the simulation, in a fruitless search for some new outcome, hoping for some slice of oblivion.

Nine.

Pickles and the Nine Vee
(A Scroungers Story)
Mark Teppo

The feral lay on the hood of the crushed vehicle, its golden fur shining in the afternoon sun. The tip of its tail twitched from time to time, the only indication that the beast was alive. Pickles knew such stillness was a ruse; the feral wasn't as insensate as it appeared. If any critter dared to creep the abandoned store behind the ruined vehicle, it would be in for a fatal surprise.

"We could sneaky-sneak around the back," one of the otter-kin was saying when Pickles found them tucked beneath the leafy shrubbery.

"It's shut," he said. He had already done a reecee. You always check the back.

"Topsies?" asked the other otterkin. "Vents and tubes?"

"How are you going to climb up top?" Pickles asked.

The pair were young, their fur still dappled in spots. They wore simple jerkins that left their arms and legs free. They were litter-mates; they had their mother's eyes and round cheeks. One was a few semis taller than the other and a bit rounder. The shorter one had a patch of white fur on his snout. It made him look like he was sporting half a mustache.

"You don't look like climbers," Pickles said.

"Nor do you," said the taller one.

"Kind of bent," said the shorter. He immediately looked mortified that he had spoken ill of an elder.

Pickles let it pass. "Which of you two is in charge?" he asked.

The question confused the otterkin; they tucked their heads together and talked with their paws. Pickles wasn't as old—or as daft—as they thought he was, and he knew some of the sign language of the otterkin. He turned his head so he wouldn't stare, but not so much that he couldn't watch out of the corner of his eye. He knew how to keep secrets. Secrets about where to find good scrounge. Secrets of other kin. Secrets about words and diagrams and scheemas.

Like the one he carried in his pack. It was for a special device that would decode the weather signals. All he needed was a power source. One of the old fuel cells—a nine vee. They used to be everywhere—falling out of drawers, lined up on the Fastie Food shelves. But, like everything else made by mankind, they had a shelf life. And now, well, the shelves were all bare, weren't they? No more trucks. No more restocking. The supply chain was broken.

He had paid a lot of shiny to learn about this place. The magpie had promised he'd find nine vees here. *Ripe for the plucking,* the bird had said. *Ripe! Ripe!*

Pickles had suspected the bird wasn't telling him everything—maggies were notorious liars, after all—and he hadn't been terribly surprised to find feral sign when he had approached the ruined building. No, the surprise had been the pair of otterkin hiding in a narrow scree of shrubbery. They had been arguing about how to get past the large feral who lived in the lot.

"What if we did a loopsie doopsie?" The otterkin were done talking among themselves.

Pickles raised an eyebrow. "Which of you two gets to be the doopsie?" he asked.

The tall one pointed at the short one, and the short one pointed at the tall one. Pickles sighed. "And therein lies the answer to my earlier question."

"Which question?" the tall one asked.

Pickles squinted at the pair. "What are you called?"

Their names were—well, their names were like all things otterkin: overly complicated and absurdly hyphenated. When they were done explaining their names, he nodded and silently dubbed them "Smug" and "Dug."

"She'll eat you both," he said, returning the conversation to the feral slumbering on the machine metal.

"She?" Smug—the taller one—sucked in his cheeks. "That's a hard lady?"

"Aye," said Pickles. "The hardest."

The otterkin peered at the slumbering feral, and Dug pressed himself closer to the ground, trying to appear smaller. "No doopsie," he muttered.

"Yeah," Pickles said. "We ain't running a decoy on her. She's just going to run you down and gut ya."

Smug ran his hands down his jerkin. "I like my guts," he said.

"Me, too," said Dug.

Pickles rubbed the back of his paw against his jaw, feeling the rough scar tissue on the back of his paw. "Gotta figure an offering," he said.

"A what?"

"A how?"

They weren't the daftest otterkin he had ever met. Usually, the water-running, slippery-furred ones were like bumblebees in a glass jar. Nothing but buzz-buzz-buzz. Big-eyed wonderment and constant movement. As easily distracted by a pebble as by a moonbeam. They had what wizards called "Near-Zero Object Permanence Retention," which basically meant they couldn't remember a fucking thing from moment to moment. Great fodder. Shitty for long-term planning. Probably why they proliferated so readily after the Scattering. No critter saw them as a threat, and, well, they were awfully cute.

All of which begged a Big Question: What were this pair doing so far out in the Ranges?

Life was full of Big Questions, however, and not all of them needed answering. Right now, he had other things on his mind.

"Moar?"

Pickles frowned at the honorific. "Pickles," he said. "I'm called 'Pickles.'"

"Moar Pickles?"

Pickles shook his head. "I'm not—just 'Pickles.'"

Smug looked at Dug, who shrugged like he didn't understand what the old badger was fussing about. "Do we need some kind of squirmy?" Smug asked. "Will she let us pass if we give her a snack?"

"I like snacks," Dug said.

Smug nodded in happy agreement. "Snacks are good," he said.

"We should have had snacks before we left this morning," Dug said. He patted his belly. "I'm a bit grumbly."

Smug wrinkled his snout. "Weren't no fry in that stream," he said. "Nothing but skeeter pods."

"Might have been some—"

"Yes," Pickles interjected, interrupted what was clearly a running routine between the pair. "Some kind of offering."

Smug and Dug were quiet for a moment, and when Pickles didn't say anything, the otterkin exchanged glances. Smug's paws danced and tapped against his chest. Dug nodded sagely. "A snack," he said proudly. "We should get her a snack."

Pickles sighed and closed his eyes. "Yes," he said, keeping his voice calm. "Some kind of snack."

Dug had a gleam in his eye. Pickles knew he wasn't thinking about the feral and the treasures she guarded. He was thinking about tasty things that would make his belly happy.

Aren't we all, pup, Pickles thought. He had punched a new hole on his belt the other day, tightening it another notch to keep his kit from slipping. Winter was coming. He could feel it in his right hip, a cold brittleness that ached all day when he slept too hard on that side. Pickles eyed the sun-warmed feral, and felt a bit mopey. He was definitely getting long in the tooth. Some day—sooner than later—a storm would lay a blanket of snow over him and he wouldn't wake.

Pickles wasn't ready for the long nap. Not yet. There were buckets yet unfilled, as Saffron used to say. *Wake up, old codger, wake up.* She would poke him in the morning—oh, so eager to violate the old saying about badgers—*the day is fresh and there are buckets to fill.*

What buckets? he would ask, grumpily rubbing away the night from his eyes.

These buckets, she would reply, tapping her head and her heart.

A murder of crows flecked the sky, and one of their number tumbled to the old pavement of the parking lot. The crow pecked at something that had caught its eye, its beak *tock-tock-tocking* against the old stone. The remainder of the murder swept around and speckled an oak at the verge of the lot with their number. They croaked at the solitary fool, who ignored their cries. *Tock-tock-tock* went his beak.

What the beans is he digging at? Pickles wondered.

The otterkin were like old stones, stuck in the muddy riverbank. Dug looked like he was holding his breath.

On the sun-warmed car carcass, the feral's tail stopped twitching.

The crow hopped widdershins, trying to get a better angle at the thing stuck in the cracks. *Tock-tock—*

There was a flash of gold, like the sun had spangled their eyes with its skirts, and all that remained of the crow was a single feather. It drifted to the ground, landing between the enormous paws of the feral. She had—in a sinuous blur—risen, leaped, and gobbled up the unwary crow.

The murder leaped into the air, screaming farewells to their fallen fellow, and the feral watched them fly away. Her eyes were a startling blue.

Dug let out a tiny squeak, and Smug covered his kin's mouth with his paws.

Pickles gripped his stick and waited.

The feral's jaw moved once, twice, as she swung her head from side to side. Her nose drank in the scents of the lot, and Pickles tensed, wondering if the wind would betray their location. It didn't, and after a moment, the feral pirouetted and leaped back to the sun-warmed hood of the metal carcass. She spat up the mangled body of the crow. She held it between her paws and looked around the open lot one last time. Satisfied she was alone, she began to eat.

"I might spew," Dug whispered.

"Away," Pickles hissed. "Get back to the trees and dig a hole. Don't let her get a whiff."

Dug looked even greener, and Pickles waved at Smug to get the ill otterkin moving. Smug nudged and pushed his kin, and the pair of otterkin slunk off for the woods, leaving Pickles alone in the scree. He stayed and watched.

He was a wild critter. He was no stranger to the savagery of the Ranges; in fact, he had done such acts of his own. He had seen pack hounds fight over a kill. Now that was real savagery. In comparison, watching a feral devour a crow was like watching one of those video loops about Mac 'n' Cheese. Eating out of a bowl. Using a plastic fork. So dainty. Not making a mess at all. Scraping the bowl clean. Every last bit.

"An offering," he muttered to himself. "Got to find an offering."

He was going to have to talk to a wizard.

In a hole in the ground there lived a wizard. Not a wet, stinking, fetid hole with the bones of who knows what poking out of the wall, nor a tight squeeze that only a shrew could navigate. It was a hole at the base of a rocky scree, and it had a nice wooden door with a brass knocker. Such a door, in such a place, meant this was a wizard-hole, and that meant learned discourse.

Back before, when the seas swarmed the shores and the sun dipped low and set the forests on fire, human folk had scampered. No one knew where to—no one really cared either, frankly; critterkind were happy to see the stenchy ones go. They left everything behind, like they always did when small groups of them ventured into the woods for a weekend, though this time, it was on a much more massive scale. When it became abundantly clear they weren't coming back, the critters started poking around the detritus of human civilizations. Those first few generations after the Scattering were hard and bleak, as critterkind fought over the scraps. It got real dark when rats learned to read and discovered the true depths of the smear campaign humanity had waged against them.

Anyway, it was the marmots who built the Gnostic Know-Now of the Holy Words. They anointed a college of saints—RayBee, JamesTee, UrsuaLee, to name a few—and avowed lessons gleaned from the biblios of these august figures. Primus among these was the Preservation of the Words. Following the scriptural warning of RayBee, each marmot took a holy oath to memorize a section of the OED, that vast catalog of all the Words.

Well, not *all* the Words. Pickles had heard stories of other tongues, spoken in other places, but those places were far, far away. Even if he started walking toward that spot where the sun leaped into the sky every morning, and he walked all day long for each of the days remaining in his life, he doubted he would arrive at one of those other places. Thinking about such distances made his head hurt; it was best to not dream about such impossible things.

But we can dream such things, Saffron used to say. Isn't that enough? Isn't that impetus enough to try? What a bucket that would be to fill!

Pickles had had quite enough talk of buckets. The one she left behind—the one he carried in his heart—had a hole in it, and no matter what he put in it, it never filled.

"Should we knock?" Smug asked Dug. The otterkin were arguing over who was brave enough to approach the wizard's door.

"Not too loudly," Dug said. "We wouldn't want to disturb anyone."

"Probably better to not knock at all," Smug said.

"Yes, yes. That is the best approach."

Smug scratched his head. "But . . . How does the wizard know we are here if we don't knock?"

"Maybe he already knows," Dug offered.

Smug ducked his head. "Is his evil eye roaming? Where is it? Do you spy it?"

"So many rocks," Dug said. "So many nooks."

"He's not watching," Pickles said. He brushed past the otter-kin and banged the brass knocker. Startled by the noise, the otterkin switched places, sinuously swarming in that instinctive way of water dogs. Pickles eyed them, and the pair stared back. Dug fumbled with an imaginary rock.

He should have left them at the lot. He would have, in fact, but they had looked so confused, so adrift. *You're not like the others,* Saffron had said. *You have . . .* She didn't know the word, but she had made a gesture with her paws, cupping them against her body.

A latch lifted, and the wooden door creaked open, revealing a white-robed figure wearing a tinsel-trimmed cap. A pair of silver-rimmed, dark-glassed spectacles hid the wizard's eyes. "What?" the wizard croaked. "Oh," he said, noticing Pickles. "You."

"Yeah," Pickles said. "Me."

The wizard looked at the pair of otterkin. "Companions?"

"Followers," Pickles said.

The wizard clucked his tongue. "Tricky," he said. "And dangerous."

"Such is life," Pickles replied. "*Quod erat demonstrandum.*"

The wizard snorted. "No one likes a fancy-tonguing badger."

"All the more reason to wag it," Pickles said.

The wizard lowered his glasses, revealing a pair of brown eyes. "They polite-like?"

Pickles looked at the otterkin. "Don't fiddle with the wizard's stuff," he said.

"No fiddling," Smug said.

"Not us," Dug echoed. His paws continued to twitch.

The wizard watched the otterkin for a moment. "He's going to fiddle," he said.

Pickles gave him a *What can you expect of otters?* shrug.

"Fine," the wizard sighed. He waved at them to follow him.

Pickles indicated the otterkin should enter the hole, and the pair danced around each other for a moment, trying to not be first. It took a low growl from Pickles to get them to commit, which turned into a bit of slapstick as they both tried to enter at the same time. There was some squawking and pushing—

Pickles considered booting one of them in the rump to facil-
itate things—but they managed to single-file their way into
the hole.

Pickles pulled the door shut behind him, and the latch
fell into place with a *clack*. The hall was dark and cool, and
in that shade, he felt the weight of the word Saffron hadn't
known. With a deep sigh, he padded after the otterkin and
the marmot.

The marmot—Weft to his warrenkin, Most Illuminous and
Extraordinarily Voluminous to the small critters who made
pilgrimages to leave berries and nuts at his door, and Partlet
Dash Partridge-Berry to other deacons of the Gnostic Know-
Now—made tea, and they all sat semi near the fire in the
warren's surprisingly sizable common area. A metal flue
corralled the smoke from the fire, and the room was quite
cozy. Smug, who hadn't liked the way the tea smelled, was
dozing. Dug was waiting for his to cool, and the waiting was
hard for the curious otterkin. He was edging toward a nearby
shelf where all manner of trinkets and feathers were collected.

"How goes the scrounge?" the wizard asked.

Pickles opened his pack and pulled out a few things. A shard
of blue plastic. A rusted spring. A scrap of material that wasn't
natural. A writing stick with its chewy end gnawed off. The
wizard admired the writing stick, and Pickles indicated he
should keep it.

"No, no," the wizard protested.

"Ain't got a way to sharpen it," Pickles said.

The wizard tasted the wooden end. "Still got lead," he said.

"Let me gift it," Pickles said. "Use it for doctrine writing."

The wizard inclined his head. "I am working on a treatise," he said. "Copying a JamesTee parable."

Pickles nodded. "The one about the dog?"

"They all have dogs in them," the wizard said. "Polite and friendly."

"Strange tales," Pickles said.

The Scattering had changed everything, and for many critterkind, the new way was the only way. The Primus Rule in the Ranges was an absolute: adapt or die. You couldn't go back to the way things were. You moved on. You ate. You slept. You scrounged. That was life. But among the proliferate texts left behind by man, there were many stories about domestics—critters who lived in community with man. Horses, goats, dogs, and cats. Some birds, too. In all these stories, dogs were special. They were bound to man, heart to heart, and in many tales, they were life mates.

These life mates were abandoned in the Scattering, and such was their sorrow that their hearts shriveled, like grapes caught in an early frost. Their pups had no masters but their own pack mates. They had no use for trust anymore. All that remained was the law of the pack, and there was no greater threat on the Ranges than the roaming pack.

Well, except for the solitary feral. They were worse.

"Got me a conundrum," Pickles said, getting around to the purpose of his visit.

Beside him, Smug snorted in his sleep. Over at the shelf, Dug started and dropped the trinket he had been fiddling with. He froze, thinking no one would notice him. The wizard gave him a stern glance over the rim of his spectacles.

"What sort of conundrum?" the wizard asked.

"There's a park-n-lot," Pickles said. "Down beyond the interchange. You know it?"

The wizard nodded. "Lots of lots past the interchange."

"This one had a convenience on it, once upon a time."

"Mayhap." The wizard leaned forward. "Heard it was scrounged out."

"Everything's been scrounged out," Pickles said. "Once or twice already."

"True, true." The wizard slurped his tea.

At the shelf, Dug had moved on to fiddling with the feathers.

"A maggie told me there might be batteries."

The marmot laughed a very marmot-like laugh. "Batteries? You heard this from a magpie? And you believed it?"

"Gotta believe in something," Pickles said gruffly, and his words made the marmot choke on his mirth.

"Aye," the wizard said when he had recovered his composure. "Belief is a mighty thing."

Dug, accidentally tickling his own nose with a feather, sneezed. Smug started awake, and his paw knocked over his tea cup. The tea made a dark stain on the rug. The wizard looked at the stain and sighed.

"Sorry," Pickles said. Mostly to be polite.

"It's fine," the wizard said. Even though it wasn't.

Smug worried his paws together, not quite sure what he had done but pretty sure someone was angry with him.

"What's the conundrum?" the wizard asked.

"There's a feral."

"Ah."

"Yeah."

"That's a mighty conundrum."

"I was hoping you might have an idea."

"For getting past a feral?"

Pickles looked at Dug, who had tucked a feather down the collar of his jerkin. It was canary yellow and twice as long as any such bird had grown. The feather was like an eye-catcher, waving back and forth like that.

The wizard was looking at the otterkin too, a thoughtful expression on his face.

"No," Pickles said. "I'm not offering a doopsie."

"Why not? They're only followers. They're not—"

"Not going to do it." Pickles put his tea cup down angrily. "Doesn't matter who they are. It's not my way." He thumped his chest. "I've got—" He looked away so the wizard couldn't see the way the word was caught in his throat.

"Empathy," the wizard said, speaking the word Saffron hadn't known. The word she had signed, cupping her paws around her heart.

"Yeah," Pickles said. "I got a big beater."

The wizard didn't say anything more. He merely sipped his tea and stared politely at the fire.

Smug wiped his nose. He glanced down and finally noticed the spilled tea. Nervously, he looked about. He grabbed a nearby throw pillow and put it over the stain. Pleased with his problem-solving skills, he ambled over to Dug, who was definitely rearranging the wizard's trinkets.

"Well," the wizard offered after awhile. "Perhaps that is the path. You should consider what's in the feral's heart."

"What do you mean?"

"Every critter wants something," the wizard said. "That's what the saints tell us. The heart of every story is what someone wants. You want to get into that shop. Those two"—he indicated the otterkin—"want snacks. That cat wants—"

"Snacks!?" Dug's attention snapped to the wizard. "There are snacks?"

"I like snacks," Smug added.

The wizard didn't bother stating the obvious.

"Conflict comes from crossings," the wizard said. "You want *this*. She wants *that*. Your paths collide." He set his cup down and banged his paws together. "Conflict!"

"I already know that," Pickles groused. "And that's what I don't want. Conflict. I want to avoid that."

"It is not possible." The wizard made a sign with his paw and put his paw to his forehead. "That's what RayBee tells us in—"

"Don't quote—" Pickles clenched his teeth and let a growl reverberate in his chest. "Reading isn't doing," he said carefully. "We did fine before the Scattering. We—"

"We didn't," the wizard countered. "Quite often we were hungry. Quite often we were afraid. Quite often we died."

"No snacks!" Dug said.

Pickles gathered up his scrounge and shoved it back in his pack. "Keep the writing stick," he said. "And thanks for the tea." He shouldered his bag and started for the front door. He didn't look back, and when he reached the door, he heard the wizard chatter at the otterkin. "Shoo! Shoo!" Pickles opened the door and went out of the warren. He stood beside the door, waiting for the otterkin, who came tumbling out a few moments later. Pickles shut the door before he had to listen to any last pointless platitude from the wizard, and the latch fell with a distinct gravitas.

Smug worried an imaginary rock. "We didn't get a snack," he said.

The yellow feather was still stuck down Dug's jerkin. He felt it tickle the back of his head, and when he turned around, the feather ducked out of his sight. He turned around again, and it tickled him once more.

"Hold still," Pickles said before the otterkin made everyone dizzy. The otterkin complied, and Pickles plucked the feather free.

"Magic!" Dug shouted.

"It was—"

"Sleighty-paws!"

"I did no magic—" Pickles shook his head.

It was a seagull feather. It had been painted, and the paint made the barbs stiff and brittle. The end of the shaft has been sharpened. It was too soft to be an effective weapon, but he supposed it would suffice as a scribble stick, should the need arise.

Pickles looked at the otterkin, who were staring at him with cutesy-doe eyes. "It was stuck in his—" He indicated the collar of his own sleeveless garment. The otterkin followed the motion of his paws, still agog with wonderment about how he had produced the feather. *Near-Zero Object Permanence Retention,* he thought. "It doesn't matter," he finished.

"Are we going back to the park-n-lot, Moar Pickles?" Dug asked.

"Sure," Pickles said. "Why not?" He felt like he was trapped in a cycle he couldn't break free from. Like one of those stories the wizard had spoken of. A fable told in the olden days. A morality tale that existed solely to terrify pups and kits into obedience. *This is the way the world ends,* he thought, remembering a line he had seen scratched on a ruined wall.

What does that mean? he had asked Saffron.

It has no meaning beyond what we give it, she had whispered.

What does that *mean?* he had meant to ask her, but before he could, she was gone.

He slipped the feather in his pack, and even though he knew it was hollow, it made his pack feel heavier.

The journey back to the park-n-lot would take longer than the remaining daylight. Pickles scouted at the base of the rockfall for some shelter, and he found a niche deep enough for all three of them. While the otterkin foraged for snacks in a nearby creek, he cleared out the cruft from the hole and padded the harder spots with leaves. The otterkin brought back a handful of shoots and roots. They wouldn't look him in the eye, and it wasn't long before Dug admitted that they had eaten the fry they had caught.

Pickles absolved the otterkin's guilt, and thus assuaged, the pair squirmed into the niche. They wrestled for awhile, complaining about pokey bits and lumps, but by the time the moon rose, they had settled down. Pickles packed himself in last so that he could crawl out and make water if he needed to during the night. One of the pair snored and the other one kept swimming in his sleep. For an hour or two, Pickles found them annoying, and he grumbled to himself about the bother.

He should have ignored them at the lot. Their natural curiosity would have tugged them out of hiding, and the feral would have played with them, batting them about for awhile before slicing open their bellies. One of them might have run, and she would have let him get a head start, but she would have chased him down. When the hunt was in the blood, there was no escape. And maybe—possibly—while she had been gutting and chasing, he could have slipped into the shop and searched the shelves for a nine vee battery.

Dug's paws sleepy-slapped against Pickles's back, and he made tiny chattering noises. Happy noises. Full belly noises.

Pickles glowered at the moon, who winked back at him.

Every critter wants something, the wizard had said. What did the feral want? That was the secret motion of the tale. What did the otterkin want? Pickles grimaced and rubbed the back of his scarred paw. What did he want?

"Buckets," he whispered, and out in the short grass of the field, a cricket chirped. She was always talking about buckets. And when he had scrounged one for her—an old dun-colored container with a hole poked in the bottom—she had laughed with delight. *Not this sort of bucket,* she had said. *But I will treasure this one forever.*

She had worn it like a lightshade, and it came down over her eyes. She bumped into things as she chased him, and they had both laughed until their cheeks were damp with tears. *It is a glorious bucket,* she had whispered that night as they spooned beneath a quilt of dry leaves. *It is what I have always wanted.*

Pickles took the weather signal box out of his pack. He fiddled with the dial and clicked the switch a few times. Nothing happened, and nothing would—not until he got a battery and fitted it into the compartment in the back. Then, according to the scheema, when he clicked the switch, a light would bloom inside the box, and when he turned the dial, a rod would move and voices would come out of the box.

And one of those voices would be hers.

With a sigh, Pickles returned the box to his pack. It did him no good to fiddle with the box. Not until he got a nine vee. He grabbed the yellow feather and tried to smooth the barbs together. It was an empty exercise, but kept his paws busy. He needed to fiddle with something. Badgers were restless critters, more so as they aged, and he had become very restless indeed.

Eventually, he fell asleep, and during his slumber, he managed to dream.

In the morning, his face was damp with dew and his bones were sore from being crammed in a hole with a pair of squirmy otterkin. He crawled out of the sleeping spot and did exercises until his joints no longer popped. He tugged his pack out of the hole and stood for a moment, watching the pair. They were wrapped around each other, like flexy-spoons that had been melted by the sun. Dug's head was supported by Smug's leg, and the smaller otterkin's face was relaxed and worry-free.

This is all he wants, Pickles thought. *A warm snuggle-hole and a full belly. How simple was that? A single bucket, easily filled.*

Pickles's stomach made a noise, and he nodded in agreement. *This one is not so easily filled,* he thought. *This one wants something more.*

He shouldered his pack, and carrying the yellow feather, he left the sleeping pair and went to find the feral.

He found her washing blood off her face. She had hunted in the pre-dawn gloom, and by the time Pickles arrived, she had finished the grisly work. When he stepped into her line of sight, she paused, paw in mid-stroke across her left ear. He was farther away than the crow had been yesterday, but close enough to make her wary. He gripped the yellow feather in one paw and held his stick loosely in the other.

"You again," she said. She ran her rough tongue across the back of her paw and swiped once more at her ear.

"I wish to ask a boon," Pickles said.

"A boon?" She made a noise deep in her chest, and it didn't sound like laughter. "Why would I grant such a thing?"

"Kindness," Pickles said.

She showed too many teeth when she laughed. "What would I want of that?" she asked.

"Nevertheless," Pickles persisted.

She stared at him, and Pickles adjusted his grip on his stick. It was slippery in his paw.

"Where did you scrounge *that*?" she asked.

It took Pickles a moment to realize the feral was talking about the yellow feather. "I—" he started. "I plucked it."

"You did not."

"I did."

She stopped washing herself. She rose, like water moving backwards, and when she stretched, he was very aware of the lean strength of her frame. "I do not believe you," she said. The tip of her tail twitched dangerously.

Pickles glanced at the yellow feather. Compared to his fighting stick, it was, well, like a feather in his paw. The words didn't want to come, but he pushed them free of his throat. "I do not care if you believe me or not," he said. "It doesn't change what I have done."

She leaped off her platform. Pickles held his ground, and when she landed, he glumly noted he had misjudged her agility. *Too close*, he thought. *I was too close.* Like one of those blinded bugs that icarused into incandescence. She leaned a little and sniffed at the yellow feather. "Painted plumage," she hissed. "This is from a ceremonial bird. It did not notice your thievery. You are not as clever as you think."

Pickles shifted the tip of his stick, so the sharp end hovered near the feral's breast. "I never claimed to be," he said.

She was utterly indifferent to his weapon, and a part of him marveled at her self-centricity. So assured of her immortality. So confident of her speed. She had more lives than he, and they both knew it.

She sniffed him too, and the edge of her lip curled at what she smelled. "You are not afraid," she said.

"I am," Pickles admitted. "But I am brave too."

"Why?" She cocked her head. "Because you plucked a feather from a stuffed bird?"

Pickles shook his head. "No, because my bucket is not full."

"Your what?"

"My bucket." He jabbed at her—lightly!—with his stick. Just enough to touch her fur. "In here."

Her reaction was a blur. His wrist was turned painfully, and his stick went *clatter-clatter* on the pavement. The yellow feather waggled and fell across his face. He brushed it aside and found he was lying on his back, staring up at the sky. He drew breath, mentally checking himself for leaks or pains. He found none, and he cautiously lifted his head.

The feral had moved a few paces away. Her tail whipped back and forth, and there was a venomous light in her eyes. "You dare dangerously, badger," she spat at him.

Pickles sat up. He looked at his stick. It was too far away. She would be on him before he even got upright. The feather, however, was right beside him, and he picked it up.

The feral snarled at him, but she didn't attack.

"Nevertheless," Pickles said. "I come to ask a boon."

"What?" she snapped. "What do you want?"

He tipped the feather toward the ruined shop. "I wish to check the shelves."

"For what?"

"For a nine vee. A battery."

"A battery? You merely want to scrounge a battery?"

He nodded.

"For what purpose?"

He cast about for his pack, which had fallen off when the feral had knocked him down. "It's for a scheema I am crafting," he said. "A squawk box that will let me hear voices—"

"Whose voice?"

Pickles didn't want to say. His paw strayed to his chest.

"Buckets," the feral sighed.

"Aye," Pickles said.

She shook her head. "There's nothing in that shop," she said. "No plastic packaging. No scraps of script. No nine vee."

"I know," Pickles said. "But I need to keep looking."

"You are a fool," the feral said.

Pickles ducked his head. "Nevertheless," he said.

She stared at him for another long moment where he imagined all the ways she was thinking of gutting and slicing him. And then she raised her paw to her mouth, licked it, and went back to grooming the fur around her ear.

His knees shaking, Pickles stood. When he reached for his stick, the feral made a noise in her chest and he abandoned that idea. He worked the tip of the feather into a crack in the pavement, and it stood like a standard. He gathered up his pack, which held his box of foolish desires, and he started toward the door of the ruined shop.

"Hup! Hup!"

He turned and saw the otterkin, who had arrived at the lot during his conversation with the feral. Dug waved happily. "A flag!" the otterkin called. "Moar Pickles raised a flag!"

"Hooray for flags!" crowed Smug. "Hooray for Moar Pickles!"

Pickles swallowed a sudden lump in his throat, and he looked at the feral. "Strange kin," she said.

"Strange times," he replied.

She yawned. "I have hunted and dined," she said. She looked at the feather stuck in the pavement. "And now I have a new toy. What more could a cat want?"

"To be left alone?" Pickles tried.

She gave him a look before she could stop herself, and Pickles made a quiet promise he would never speak of what he saw in her gaze. "Run along," she said. "Before I change my mind. Before—"

Pickles whistled for the otterkin, who came, bouncing and flouncing. His pack was light on his shoulder as he turned toward the shop and its empty shelves.

Cat of Nine Tales

Jeb R. Sherrill

Ralph sauntered through the vast hallway. His well-licked tail stood almost straight but crooked at the tip. The nap had been relaxing, so naturally he'd followed it with several hours of grooming.

He gave a deep sigh which turned to a low growl as he noticed the door. Ralph couldn't imagine why Ted had left the stupid thing shut. Why did humans close doors anyway? Why bother having them at all? They just got in your way. They stopped the air from circulating. Barred him from his damn food.

Ralph slipped into Ted's room and hopped up on the dresser. His servant's prized karate trophy perched just above the trash. Nah. He shook his head. Too obvious. Too easy.

A picture of Ted's girlfriend stood just beside the trophy. It was in a glass frame. Ralph brushed by both objects just enough to make them rock back and forth a bit, but not enough to fall.

Cliché.

A roll of Ted's prized Charmin perched on the edge of his end table so he could blow that monstrous nose of his in the middle of the night when Ralph was trying to sleep.

Please. A cat tearing up toilet tissue? Like that hadn't been done to death and back.

He hopped up on the bed and kneaded his claws into the soft cotton of the top blanket. There were rules to these things. Punishments. Consequences.

Shutting the door to Ralph's food bowl was not a capital offense in and of itself. However, shutting the door to his food not two days after allowing the water to run dry until morning—three days after allowing a bald spot the size of a half dollar to appear in the middle of the food bowl—four days after not only running the soul-sucking, cat-eating, reprehensible *vacuum of doom*, but allowing it into the sanctum sanctorum beneath the bed—and only one day after rolling over in the middle of the night when he knew good and well Ralph was sleeping on Ted's back—and later evicting the weary cat from the bed after a mild but admittedly sharp attack upon Ted's feet . . .

Ralph realized he had trailed off as he seethed within. All in all, it was about time Ted was reminded just what Ralph kept him around for. Heaven knows it wasn't his good looks. Each time the idiot took off his fur, the imbecile exposed his hairless, rubbery body to eyes which should never have to endure such things. Ted's girlfriend was just as bad.

Several sniffs and a scratch here and there brought him to just the spot Ted generally laid his naked rump. Ralph turned several times and pushed his rear end deep into the crocheted throw which lay across Ted's side of the bed. If Ralph did this right, the incompetent fool wouldn't see the wet spot until it was too late. He'd have no idea until he slid beneath the sheets and into the damp circle he always met with such stark horror. If he was passed out drunk, Ted might even fall asleep in it and wake to the harsh smell of ammonia the next morning.

Ted would yell and scream at Ralph for a good ten minutes as he went for new sheets. The yelling was actually the fun part, and there would be little true retribution. If the incompetent creature really wanted to punish the cat, he'd stay at home all the time furless and force Ralph to watch him manscape. The cat shuddered. Servants had no clue how revolting this was.

If Ralph had had either the facial muscles or the human cultural tendency to do so, he would have smiled. He hadn't peed in just over a day, saving it up in preparation for Ted's next inevitable infraction. Relaxing, he let the liquid gush. It felt so good he thought he'd gone to heaven until something beneath him went pop, pop, pop, and he . . . well . . . went to heaven.

Ralph rolled his eyes at the all-too-familiar corridor which stretched out before him. Here, he walked upright on two paws. His front paws were more articulate than in life and he wore a faded suit with a red tie.

Napoleon glared up as Ralph approached the porter's chair which stood this side of what might (or might not) have been Cat Heaven. He'd never had any interest in finding out. Napoleon was also a cat, but shorter, wearing a tattered brown suit. Less a real cat though and more like a demonic/angelic entity dredged up from the bowels of wherever the hell he'd been recruited from.

This bedraggled creature was the gatekeeper of the next realm. "That's ten," Napoleon growled in a rough north-English accent. "I told you not to pee on stuff like that. Didn't you already die pissing on a power strip when you were trying to fry Ted's computer?"

"How was I supposed to know there was an electric blanket on the bed?" Ralph said, his tone absurdly British. "And it wasn't his computer. It was the game console."

"That was number eight," Napoleon said. "Number four was the computer."

"There is no number eight. I'm still on seven."

Napoleon cocked his head. He stood up in the chair and squared his shoulders. "You were on nine, *Ralph*, and now you've reached ten."

Ralph straightened his tie and stood slightly straighter. "You, sir, have mistaken me for another cat. My sixth was when I went after a damned fish and wound up drowning." This was the moment he almost cherished. Napoleon was so easily antagonized.

"You won't pull that shit with me," the other cat said. "Number six was the time you took a shit in his girlfriend's shoe and she fell on you. Hardly the first time your little punishments have knocked you down a notch."

"It was always worth it," Ralph said. "Like the time I sniffed half his sugar, rolled in the other half, then spent the next few spastic minutes distributing it across the walls and ceiling before my heart exploded. And *that* was number three."

Napoleon rocked back on his heals and gave an exaggerated laugh. "First, that was number two. And second, that wasn't sugar. It was cocaine."

"It was good shit," Ralph proclaimed. "Beat the hell out of pixie sticks. Or was that number two?"

"The pixie sticks?" Napoleon asked. "Wasn't that number one?"

"Ah, no," Ralph said, pushing both paws into his pockets. "Number one was different." The little bureaucrat was his now.

Napoleon narrowed his sliver eyes. "I don't think I remember that one."

"Of course you don't," Ralph said, turning to pace, forcing the other cat to follow. "That was your predecessor. A Maine Coon, as I recall. Huge fucker. Scared the bejeezus out of me, the first time." Ralph gazed wistfully into the distance.

"You were saying?" Napoleon asked after four or five pregnant moments.

Ralph turned a quizzical eye on the shorter cat. "Got any nip by chance? It's been a while."

The other cat searched his pockets instinctively, "Oh, um, well . . . I," he stammered as he rummaged first through his pants, then the outside pockets of jacket and moved to the inner breast pockets. "I had a sack of fags the other day, but . . ." he said, re-ransacking his pockets, his north-English accent thickening.

"It's quite all right," Ralph said, drawing the self-same sack from his own pocket, withdrew a tightly packed cigarette and lifted it to his mouth.

Napoleon snatched the packet away. "I'd forgotten how light your paws are," he said, shoving the bag into the pocket of his jacket with a bit more force than was probably advisable considering its delicate contents. "I suppose you'll be wanting a light now?" he added, folding his arms.

"I'm fine," Ralph said with a dismissive wave, withdrawing a silver Zippo from his pocket.

"—the devil did you get that?" the short cat spat, snatching at the gleaming device.

Ralph turned his head as if he hadn't noticed, lit the catnip and drew in a lungful. He tossed the lighter over his shoulder, delighting just a bit at the sound of Napoleon scrambling to catch the smooth metal.

"You—are—a—nasty—little—shit," the cat said, drawing out the words for full effect.

"I was just a kitten really," Ralph continued, unphased. "So small. So innocent of the ways of the world."

"I doubt that," Napoleon sneered.

"Ted bought me for his girlfriend. The crazy one who made necklaces with the cleaned skulls of the mice I brought her. She liked them so much I had to quit bringing them. I mean, she didn't even scream. Where's the fun in that, I ask you?" He fixed his eyes on Napoleon as if waiting for an answer, but when the smaller cat opened his mouth, Ralph snapped his gaze away and continued.

"Oh, I was carefree in those days," he said, continuing his lazy gait as Napoleon followed away from the corridor, into the more scenic area of the In-Between. At least the grass was soft. "Destroying pillows. Devouring houseplants. Erasing hard drives by running across the right keys. I was so damned cute they didn't even yell at me. Poor bastards. I used to try and get them to put me down just so I could come up here for a breather, but alas . . ." He trailed off. "They never notice I've gone and come back, after all. Each time I come back it just resets everything."

"Anyone ever tell you you're an asshole, even for a cat?" Napoleon asked. "You nearly killed him that one time you tripped him down the stairs."

Ralph sighed. "I was bored. None of these servants are any good. Didn't want to kill the idiot without the front door open, anyway. I was this far from nibbling his eyeballs before he groaned. Besides, he'd given me dry food again. Again! How the devil is one supposed to survive on that dry, flavourless crunchy garbage. I need flesh. Flesh!"

Napoleon took an unconscious step back. "Bit of a psycho aren't ya?"

Ralph took a deep drag and blew out a thin cloud of smoke. "Is it mad to want it all?"

The other cat cleared his throat. "Are you going to tell me how you died the first time, or do I have to listen to the extended edition of your childhood memoirs?"

"Oh, that," Ralph said. "Well, I'd never seen a Christmas tree before, now had I? My God, the thing was beautiful. His girlfriend's doing, obviously. Ted couldn't decorate a macaroni collage if you didn't teach him how to get the top off the glue first."

Napoleon opened his mouth to protest something.

"But I digress," Ralph said, cutting of the other cat's objection. "The point is, I *had* to climb the damned thing, now didn't I?"

The smaller cat nodded. "I imagine that would be difficult to resist."

"Try impossible," Ralph snapped. "Glass balls. Glowing lights. A chew toy at the top with wings of coloured gossamer."

"And I suppose you decided to bite down on one of the wires, setting the entire tree on fire and nearly burning down the house?"

Ralph gave another dismissive wave as he hopped up on a rock and continued across a small plateau. "Alas, I had little knowledge of the intricacies of electric wiring at the time. No, in an attempt to swat down six glass balls in the space of less than a second, I managed to ensnare myself in a tangle of gold garland, strangling myself in the process."

"Good Lord," Napoleon said. "Don't you ever die of natural causes?"

"Natural causes?" Ralph reeled on the other cat. "Natural causes. Who wants to go down like that? Old and sickly with matted fur, pissing myself while that overgrown fool stares down at me?"

Napoleon stopped, turned and gazed about. "Where are we?" he asked, trying to get his bearings. "Have we been walking this whole time?"

Ralph grunted. "Don't you ever leave that chair and walk around?"

The smaller cat glanced about as if searching for landmarks. "I'm not really supposed to leave my chair. Don't even know what all is between the gate and . . . well . . . the door or whatever you arrived through. I trust you know the way back?" He said it with confidence, but there was an edge of fear to his voice.

The smoking cat didn't answer but sat down on the edge of a cliff overlooking a thousand-foot drop. There was no real bottom to see, though there had to be something down there, eventually. Ralph took a final drag of nip and flicked the spent butt off the rock, watching it tumble into the infinity below.

Napoleon backed away as the gravity of his situation sank in. "They'll miss me and come after you."

"Funny," Ralph said, giving a toothy smile he was only capable of in this heavenly form. "I mean, it's been some odd years, but I swear your predecessor said the exact same thing."

The smaller cat searched his surroundings for a point of escape, but the way they'd come was blocked by Ralph himself and they stood in rock box of sorts atop the cliff. "That makes no sense. It was your first life. Why would you do anything like that on your first life?"

Ralph stretched, popping several vertebrae in the process. "My first life? Well, that might have been a bit of a fabrication. You see, I've been around much longer than that."

"Impossible," Napoleon said, crouching as if he might attack. "You don't get any more than nine and I've seen at least eight of them."

"Really? I've lost count," Ralph said. "Of you gatekeepers, I mean." He advanced on the smaller cat. "I meet you ten times each, in general, but not always."

"This is unnatural," Napoleon pleaded. "You'll upset the order of things."

"Like the glass vase knocked off the mantle? Like pissing on a laptop? Sinking my claws into the backside of a horse just as a cowboy gets on its back? Scaring a pharaoh or two off the top steps of a pyramid? Back when they still had decent servants."

Napoleon's eye grew wide. "You're *that* cat?"

"The one and only," Ralph/Ralpheneus/Ralpheum/Raffime said, closing in. "Nine is simply not enough."

☆

Ralph spread out on Ted's bed wondering if the pillow might work as a better pee spot from now on. Electric blankets were a hateful addition indeed. Besides, the door was open now. He had eaten his fill and the wet food had satiated him for the moment. If Ted kept his nose clean, Ralph might not have to take a crap on his chest again as he slept.

But that was a big *if*.

The Park Trolls

Andrew W. McCollough

On a clear Sunday afternoon in September Billy's dad took him and Scruff to feed the trolls under the footbridge down by the duck pond in the park.

"I heard they're like goldfish, they can only get as big as the bridge they are under, Dad!" Billy said.

"Really? That's interesting." Dad took out his cell phone and looked at it.

"Hey, Dad," Billy said, and shook the crumpled bag of troll treats in his hand. It was just some leftover dog food, but trolls loved it. "Do you think we'll see the one with the hooks?" Scruff nosed his hand, asking for some kibble. He had just been fed but that didn't matter to Scruff.

"The old bull? Maybe. That one has been around since I was your age." Dad stopped by the water and sat down on a bench overlooking the water. "Why don't you go ahead, Billy, I'm going to have a quick smoke." He tapped at his phone some more.

Billy left Dad at the bench and headed up the winding path along the duck pond, leading Scruff on his leash. Fall had left piles of leaves raked into neat piles and Scruff spent as much time as possible nosing into each until Billy tugged on his leash. Eventually, they reached the bridge, a single low arc over the thin stream that fed the duck pond, and Billy stepped out onto it. His feet made *tappity-tap-tap* sounds as he walked across.

He was halfway over when one, then another, tiny troll head peeked over the side of the bridge. A moment later a third popped out, rubbing sleep and what looked like pigeon feathers out of its eyes. All three of them, making a triangle around his scabby nose.

Scruff barked his sharp puppy bark and hid behind Billy's legs.

"Who's that tramping over my bridge?" said the biggest troll, about the size of a spaniel on its hind legs, with a nose like a broken stick.

"It's just me, Billy! And Scruff."

"We're coming out to gobble you up!" said the smaller troll, about the size of a cat. It picked at a broken shaft of horn jutting from the side of its head with a yellow claw. He looked like a Stubby, and Billy almost laughed.

But then Billy felt the troll magic curl around his legs like a lizard's tongue, gripping, tugging, holding him in place. Scruff barked frantically, but the puppy couldn't move either. Billy got scared; trolls always got fed, one way or another, and they weren't particular. But then he remembered the treats and shook the bag of kibble.

Seven bloodshot troll eyes fastened on the bag. "Is that for us?" said the biggest troll. Billy decided to call him Broke-nose.

"Don't gobble me up, have some troll treats instead," said Billy.

"Well, OK," squeaked the smallest troll, about the size of a squirrel, dragging a leathery tail with bedraggled tuft of wiry hair on the end. Rat-tail, for sure.

Billy gave each troll a handful of dog food.

"Can we have some more?" said Broke-nose.

"I don't have any more."

"Well then, we'll gobble you up!" they said in chorus.

"If you eat me up, then I can't come back with more treats," said Billy, shaking the bag, "And then you'll have to just keep eating . . . whatever you've been eating under there."

"Squirrels, mostly," said Stubby, scratching its pondscum hide.

"And pigeons. Lots of pigeons. It's been pigeons every day for a month now," said Rat-tail. He pulled a wet feather from his mouth and threw it on the bridge. Scruff sniffed at it and winced back, scraping at his nose with a forepaw. Billy yanked his leash again.

"That sounds nasty. But if you let me go I'll bring back more delicious treats."

The trolls huddled on the bridge like a pile of cow flops, muttering. Then Broke-nose stepped forward, showing a smile like he'd drunk vinegar. "We'll let you go if you swear to bring treats next time."

"It's a deal!" said Billy, and it was. Even at ten Billy knew the dangers of breaking a deal, much less breaking a deal with the Fair Folk. They spit on the ground together and it was done, the magic wrapped around his legs released him slowly, as if committing his taste to memory. The trolls vanished over the edge of the bridge, leaving a whiff of methane and a yellow slick of mucous behind.

Billy ran off the bridge and around the lake with Scruff until he found his father lazily smoking and deep in conversation on his phone.

"I saw the trolls, Dad!"

"Just a sec," Dad said, "It's the kid." He glanced up. "Billy, why don't you throw rocks down by the water."

"What about lunch?"

"Soon. I'm on the phone." He raised the phone again, "Sorry, love. What were you saying? Where?"

Billy scuffed his way down to the lakeside and sat down. There was an empty trash can next to the bench and he tossed the empty kibble bag toward it, making the shot the first time. He looked around, but Dad hadn't moved and Scruff busied himself crunching leaves. Billy almost wished he'd spent more time with the trolls. At least they would talk to him.

He tossed a handful of pebbles half-heartedly at the ducks, sending them quacking indignantly away, then sat on the grass with Scruff. He wondered who Dad had been talking to. Dad never called Mom "Love."

Billy meant to come back the next Sunday to feed the trolls, but chores happened, and then the divorce, and then school got bad after a few fights with the older kids. And then it was summer and his memory of the trolls faded amid the shouting and lawyers and trips between houses until custody got settled and he moved in with Grandma while Mom looked for work.

When he eventually came back home from Grandma's, Bill lived with Mom across town and too far to walk to the troll park. Mom hated trolls. And Dad, on the fewer and fewer times Bill saw him, would rather take him to the video game arcade or the ice cream shop in the strip mall with Louise than to the park.

So by the time Bill walked Scruff through Holder Park five years later on a warm summer's evening, he had forgotten his bargain with the trolls. He and Mom had just moved in a few blocks away from Holder Park the week before and he was exploring the neighborhood. He thought he remembered an ice cream shop in the area.

Mom had been reluctant to come back to this neighborhood, and she blamed him. He'd been expelled, again, from his high school for fighting, and this district had the last high school in town that would take him. Mom never asked him why he was fighting, especially when he was so bad at it. She just said she saw his Dad in him, and that was reason enough for her.

The real reason was that the other boys called him fag and made sure that he never had more than five minutes in peace without one of them flicking him on the head, dumping water over him, tripping him, or any of a thousand petty torments.

It was no use saying anything, so he didn't. He just took it. Until finally, sometimes, he couldn't, and he fought back and lost and then it was their word, sworn up and down, against his that he'd started it. He always lost fight that too.

Scruff started whining as soon as they wandered onto the grass, then growling when they got over by the lake and started up the concrete path that wound around under the trees, until Bill jerked on his chain.

"Shut up Scruff," he said, "Just some ducks. Leave them." But Scruff kept on his growling.

Bill saw an arched footbridge up ahead and he hurried his steps, pulling Scruff to heel behind him. He liked bridges, always had. But Scruff didn't like this one and Bill had to drag him up the incline, barking all the way. It wasn't until the two trolls jumped up on the bridge that Bill remembered the last time he was here.

"Who's that trampling over my bridge!" yelled the bigger troll, about the size of a pit bull, with a curled horn as yellow as fall leaves jutting from his temple.

"It's Billy!" said the smaller one, about the size of a spaniel, his tail fluffed like a fox. "He's come back!"

"No, I haven't," said Bill. "My name's not Billy, anyway."

"Yes it is, I can always smell a promise, broken or not, and you made us a promise," said Yellow-horn. "You said you would bring us treats."

"Or get gobbled up!" said Fox-tail. Its pink tongue licked its lips and then each of its eyes.

Bill knew he was in trouble. He could feel the promise he'd made like glue on his feet, dragging at him, binding his bones. The bridge wouldn't let him leave unless he fed the trolls, one way or the other. It was old magic, troll magic, deep and instinctive, as strong and hungry as they were and impossible to escape. Bill felt it sliding over his skin like a snake's caress, tasting.

Scruff barked again, snarling, pulling at his leash to get at the trolls, but the magic held him fast as well.

"Down boy, shut up, sit, SIT!" he jerked on the chain until Scruff, whining, lay down on the bridge. The fool dog would just get himself killed, barking at them. Those trolls were as big as Scruff. Bigger. As big as Bill.

"Didn't you used to be smaller?" he said.

The two trolls looked at each other and laughed like gravel falling on concrete.

"We grew. Trolls grow when we eat lots," said Yellow-horn. "And we ate lots!"

Fox-tail scratched the gleaming scales on his belly. "There sure was a lot of Gristle!"

"There were three of you last time," he said. "What happened to the other one?"

Yellow-horn's smiled gleamed like a broken bottle under the sodium lights. "We ate him."

"We found a runaway dog." Fox-tail bounced closer on his sharp toes. "And Gristle ate and ate until he fell asleep. But he didn't let us have any, so we strangled him with the leash and ate them both up." Fox-tail's eyes glowed like three red moons rising over the oozing crater of his nose.

"Oh." Bill didn't know what to say to that.

"But that was a long time ago. I'm hungry again," said Yellow-horn. "Where are the treats you promised?"

"I don't smell any treats." Foxtail sniffed the air, "I just smell Billy, and dog, and an old stick of cinnamon gum. No troll treats. NO TREATS!"

Both trolls jumped up and down on the bridge until it shuddered under them. Scruff whined again, but Bill yanked hard on his choke collar.

"Stop, stop!" said Bill, his throat tight, "You're right, I don't have treats with me. I left them at my house, just a couple of blocks away. I can go and get them and be right back in ten minutes. Ok?"

"NO," said both trolls together. "Treats now or Billy now."

"Five minutes? I will run, I'll be right back, I promise."

The trolls stopped jumping and huddled, muttering, a pile of leprous rocks. They scrabbled closer, mouths gaping like twin sewer drains.

Yellow-horn grinned, white teeth sharp as broken coke bottles. "Last time you left and didn't come back for years and years. And when you did come back you didn't bring the treats. You lied."

"So we will let you get the treats, just ten minutes. But you have to leave the dog."

Bill looked down at Scruff. The dog had stopped whining but his tail was close to his body, not wagging. He was breathing heavily. Scruff was scared.

"No, I can't leave Scruff. He's my dog. I raised him from a pup." Bill reached down and Scruff snuffled his hand. "You can't have him."

Foxtail clacked his teeth, together, chittering, "We don't want him, we don't want a nasty dog pooping under our bridge. We will keep him until you come back. Then you can have him."

"I don't, no. No, I won't."

"Then we're going to gobble you UP, Billy!" said the trolls and laughed a rattling, clattering laugh. And it was true, Bill could feel it. He'd made a promise and broken it and they were stronger and bigger. The magic slithered up both legs, dragged over his belly and began tightening around his throat. They had the right to gobble him up. And they would.

The trolls came closer, closer, until their teeth snapped in
his face. He couldn't run, couldn't fight, couldn't breathe.
"We're going to gobble, gobble, gobble you UP." Bill felt Scruff
hiding behind his suddenly wet, shivering legs. The trolls'
cold breath against his cheek smelled of algae and wet dog.

"NO!" Bill shouted, and threw Scruff's leash at the trolls.

Ever after, in those few times he could bear to think of that
moment, he saw the leash curling in the air, heard the troll's
snapping, crackling laughter, and felt the cold sick in his belly
curdle. Worse, though, was Scruff's choked whine when the
trolls jerked the leash and pulled him close.

Bill heard Scruff barking and barking almost to the side-
walk that surrounded the park. And though Bill ran down
the wide, winding paths as fast as he could, all the way home
and back—panting and out of breath—to the bridge in ten
minutes or less, no more than fifteen, with a full bag of
kibble, the trolls wouldn't come out. No matter how much he
stomped and shouted and shook the bag with the treats. No
matter how long he sat on the bridge holding the chewed-off
end of Scruff's leash.

Bill never told anyone what happened, just said Scruff ran
away. He never got another dog, either, no matter what Mom
wanted. He couldn't bear it. He started running track and at
least the boys at the new school didn't bully him much. He
was faster than any of them, after a while, and they never
caught him again.

☆

William came back to Holder Park just once more, ten years later. He'd got sent home from a tour in the desert and the VA hospital was not too far from the park. He'd remembered the trolls during his stay at the hospital and he thought he'd pay them a visit. They were the only unfinished business he had in town; his few friends moved on, Mom dead of cancer while he was on deployment and Dad, well. William didn't know and didn't care.

When he got to the park he saw that the ice cream shop, that whole strip next to the park, was torn down, the dozers trundling back and forth, hardhats shouting to each other. From the billboard out front it looked like they were replacing the shops with a new mall. William didn't care one way or the other, the ice cream had never been that good anyway. William went on past and around to the lake side where the footbridge still arched over the brook.

A fence strung with "Beware of Trolls" signs cut off access to this section of the park and confirmed he'd found the right place. He pried the chain link aside with his cane and scrambled awkwardly under the fence, moving slow. His pant leg tore on the wire and tugged him to a wincing stop. The rusted wire had only scratched up the stainless steel rod but twinged his stump.

Autumn had left a year of leaves scattered, unraked, under the trees. Along the paths, a thin wind stirred the trash and sent plastic bottles scuttling across the algae-scummed lake. The narrow paths shushed and crackled underfoot as he limped toward the brook and its crossing.

His heavy boots shook the small footbridge and his cane added a lighter beat. *Thud-thud-tap, thud-thud-tap.*

"Hey trolls!" he said, and set one hand on his holster. The brown leather shone in the fading light.

There was silence from under the footbridge. William stomped on the bridge again with his good leg. "Trolls! I know you're all down there. Come out!" He unsnapped his holster and drew, holding his old service weapon by his side. He'd cleaned it just this morning and the evening light glinted blue-black from the barrel.

There was a rattle under the bridge, the sound of trash stirring around as something shuffled through it. Then a troll scrambled over the side of the bridge and crouched by the railing.

"Who, who's that tromping on my bridge?" it said, panting. Its tail hung limply to the side, a dirty rope unraveling. Its skin was pitted and yellow-green and stretched taut over its ribs. One eye leaked pus, wandered toward him then away. Scarred sockets showed where the other two had been.

"It's me, William. Bill. Billy."

"Billy? Oh, you brought me troll treats once. Did you bring treats?" The troll tried to wipe puss from his eye but only smeared a yellow streak down a flaking cheek.

"Not this time," William clenched a hand on his weapon. "Where is the other one? Yellow-horn?"

"Slobber? He died, got sick after they sprayed the park with troll repellant." The troll shrugged and its tail twitched. "But I'm still here." It slumped again. "Still here." Its head leaned against the low handrail.

"Well, too bad. I was planning on having a talk with you both."

The troll started up, tail flailing. "Did you bring treats? Like you promised?" The troll struggled to stand.

"No. No treats." William smiled, for once as hungry as the troll. "I broke my promise. No more treats." He felt the magic tug at his left foot, but found nothing to grasp on his right but cold iron. The magic felt rotten as long-buried cloth, his boot tore through and he felt it shred away.

"Ah, uh, uh," said the troll and crouched again. "Ok." It rested one hand on its pot belly and leaned over it. It was quiet except for its gasp and wheeze.

William looked at the troll for a long time while the sun faded behind the trees. He could fix this at least, this one regret. The weapon's familiar weight filled his hand, waiting. His arm tensed, his trigger-finger readied itself. No one would hear.

A mallard called down at water's edge and the sound of a dog barking and a boy laughing drifted across the lake, mingling with the scent of woodsmoke. On the other side of the park, the construction workers putting in the new mall shouted to each other as they headed home for the evening. A faint *pop-pop-pop* echoed, tensing his shoulders, but it was only fireworks.

William stood in the twilight, listening to the sounds of peace, until his shoulders relaxed and his finger uncurled.

There really wasn't any point, was there? He knew what had happened, why. No call to blame anyone else. He holstered his weapon.

Besides, he had had enough of that in the war, had gotten his own back, every sour drop. He laughed, but the air didn't leave his throat.

He closed his holster with a crisp snap. He'd made it, others hadn't, time to move on. He knelt beside the troll.

"I'm William. Do you have a name?"

The Final Waking

Jessie Kwak

They think I'm dead.

The heretics threw my body into the trash pit with the rest of the refuse—they should have burned me, but they didn't know.

My legs and neck are broken, my torso slashed open. It itches as the wound knits, my bones ache as they heal, but I know from experience that this will pass.

Ever since I took my vows I've wondered how my ninth and final waking will feel. I expected panic, but despite the trash pit, despite the state of my body, my soul is strangely peaceful. True death still terrifies me, but I thank the Goddess this is the last time I'll be revived.

I hear a chittering and open my good eye to see a spun sugar scorpion crouching over me, considering me for a meal. A drop of pure sucrose gleams opalescent on the tip of her barb, poised a hand's breadth from my pupil.

For a moment I imagine that I could startle it, take the poison lance through my skull and finally be done with this for good—I won't wake a tenth time.

But it would be a disgrace to die here on this trash heap with my Goddess unavenged.

"I'm not dead," I whisper to the scorpion and she rears up, startled. She skitters back a safe distance then waits.

"I wondered," she says finally. Her carapace shimmers in the dim light. "They should have burned your body."

"They didn't know."

She clicks one candied pincer derisively. "They don't know anything."

"Did any of my sisters survive?"

That sway to the left and then the right, it could be a shrug.

The vertebrae in my neck seem to be healed enough that I can chance sitting up, so I do, watching in fascinated horror as my shattered right shinbone snaps back into place. A miracle, some might call it. I used to think so, too. I blink, but my bad eye stays shut. It happened three lives ago, when a fight against a monsoon leopard had taken my eye along with a life from both myself and Vallizha. I keep hoping it will heal with one of these wakings.

If it didn't this final time, though, it never will.

Waking up is always the worst, but soon my bones are in place and the afterglow of rebirth begins to set in—it feels like warm gold, pooled sunshine, and I want to curl up and nap until the pain is over.

Intoxicating, yes. But beneath the glow, I'm laying in a putrid trash pit, my sisters are gone or dead, and my Goddess has been slain.

The spun sugar scorpion is still watching me.

I pull myself into a crouch; my recently-shattered shinbone holds my weight. "We must drive them out of the City," I tell the scorpion. "Will you help me?"

She laughs, a cynical hiss. "Yeah, not a chance." Her feet rattle against heaps of bone as she turns and skitters away. "Door's to your left," she calls.

I could tell her that the heretics' arrival and the Goddess' fall isn't just a problem for the Sisterhood, it spells ruin for all the strange denizens of our City—even those living in its trash pits. But I am not spending my last life arguing with a spun sugar scorpion. I search the trash heap for any other survivors before I go, but find nothing but rot and filth. I know some of my sisters were on their last lives—I can't think of watching Vallizha die her final time or I'll collapse into grief. But surely not all. Surely I will find some of them in the City.

I finally crawl through the door the spun sugar scorpion pointed out, then unsheath my claws to scale the City wall and find my revenge.

The heretics came in with the first fall thunderstorm, sailing over the City's walls with the lightning and splashing into the cobbled streets in gouts of rain. The storm was violent and impassible; the battle was the same.

The Sisterhood fought tooth and claw, but the heretics took us by surprise, slashes of lightning illuminating flashing swords. The temple doors had been battered down as much by the wind as the heretics's clubs, shards of shattered stained glass and hails of barbed arrows falling over us one and the same. The black pools on the ancient mosaic floors were rainwater or blood or both.

The Goddess' roar of agony as the heretics lassoed her with razorwire and pulled her to onto their forest of spears must have shaken the entire City. But if my sisters and I screamed as we died, no one could have heard us over the thunder and rain.

By daylight I can see that the heretics are only humans, and their numbers are less than impressive. Why have they come? Maybe they think our City is an abomination because it is a refuge for non-humans and those of us who chose to become something more than human to serve the Goddess. Maybe they serve a rival god. Maybe they are simply looking to loot the temple for treasure.

The heretics have set up camp in the temple. Taking prayer rugs for bedrolls, breaking apart the altar for their cookfires, pissing in the holy garden. They're drinking wine out of reliquaries which used to contain the eyeteeth and claws of sainted sisters who went before us—Vallizha will have her own if I can find her body once this is all over. The holy relics have been tossed into the same trash chute they'd thrown my body down, I can only suppose.

I sneak onto the rooftop of the market across the street to watch. They're rounding up the locals, sorting them at the temple steps. Children herded into the courtyard, the men and women judged by some metric I don't understand and loaded into carts. It's not by species, it's not by gender. It doesn't seem to be by age. As I watch, a dulmo tries to resist, spikes flaring out along his forearms and whipcord tongue snaring one of the heretics by the throat and snapping his weak human neck.

The rebellion doesn't last long. A pair of heretics release a volley of bolts from their crossbows and the dulmo's blood joins the smears that already paint the temple steps.

As the crowd screams and wails in the aftermath of the dulmo's death, I see the first flicker of hope. There. Lurking in the alley across the street is Izari. I'll always know her by the way she walks, the ferocious set to her shoulders, and the geometric tattoos scrawled on the backs of her hands.

She looks like she's about to pounce, and when she does, she'll die once more. She's lost fewer lives than me, but she can't afford to be careless, even so.

Izari crouches, knife in hand.

I *flare*.

I'm not sure it will work. In the ritual that made me part of the Sisterhood, drops of the Goddess's fiery blood burned my tongue, mingled with the blood on my sliced-open palms and kindled fire throughout every vein.

Now am I in you eternally, the Goddess had told me, *as I am in your sisters.*

It's her power that grants us the blessing and curse of our many deaths, that brings light to our eyes in the dark, that lengthens our eyeteeth, that slashes claws through our palms to be weapons and tools.

And which links all of us in the Sisterhood together.

There is no precedent for the murder of the Goddess, so I have no idea if I can still call on her powers. But I revived one last time, didn't I? Maybe, just maybe, there's hope.

Across the street, Izari stiffens. She felt my presence, and now she turns to scan the rooftops. When she spots me, she smiles, fangs bared.

Then her smile widens, and I feel it, too. Brixha's flare, from behind the temple. Ooli answering from closer to the City's walls. Nazhiimi's call, distantly faint but ready to fight.

Cloak yourselves, I whisper through our bloodlink. *And meet me on the temple steps.*

Seven of my sisters are still silent. I know for a fact that four passed the threshold the final time in the attack last night—*I cannot think about Vallizha*—but that leaves eight of us to fight.

First, though, we must get close enough.

I drape a scarf over my head, but my good eye still burns yellow, an unworthy shadow of the Goddess's own crimson flames. Once the heretics look me or any of my sisters in the eye, they'll know who we are.

A weeping venaia does a double take when she glimpses under my hood. Her doe's face goes bright with fear, then hope. Ooli grabs her arm from the other side and the venaia stifles a yelp. "Don't give us away," I hiss. "And when the fighting starts, tell the others to run." The venaia nods fiercely and clacks her hooves together beneath her robes.

They spot Brixha first, I feel her flare of fury as one of the heretics throws off her hood. She whirls with knives in hands and blood sprays from the heretic's throat. I roar and leap at a heretic who's shoving the gentle venaia toward a cart, burying my blade in his back. The venaia throws back her head and lets fly her ululating call. The heretics—and the few human citizens in the crowd—throw their hands over their ears.

The Goddess protects my formerly human ears, and I charge the temple gate after Ooli.

Two heretics go down under Ooli's blade before the first

crossbow bolt takes her through the thigh. A second buries itself in her throat.

I don't have time to mourn her final death, because a third crossbow bolt shatters against the temple steps beyond me; I felt the wind of its passing on my cheek.

I grab one of the heretics who's charging at me and spin; the fourth bolt buries itself in his back and I plunge into the temple to find safety from the archers.

The sight that greets me through the temple doors makes me stumble.

They've slain the Goddess, but they haven't been able to move her from the sanctuary. She lays on her side, fur matted with blood that has stopped flowing, though rivulets of it ran molten through the tile floor, scoring deep channels. Her ember eyes are wide open and glossy black as dead coals.

Someone screams my name, and I realize I'm gaping. I tear my gaze away from the horror of my fallen Goddess and duck the sword that whistles past where my head had just been. The swordsman swings again as I jump back, knives in my hands.

He's grinning at me, his blade black with the blood of my fellow City denizens, and of my sisters. "Die, abomination," he growls as he thrusts, and I block the blade of his sword in my crossed knives and force him back. I draw blood on his shoulder but the tip of my knife blade only sparks along the metal of his breastplate as I spin.

He swings again, and I may be faster but he has strength and a longer reach. Still, I dive in close and bury a knife in his thigh—he roars in pain and forces me back, and just as I'm about to finish him off, searing pain carves through my back. I fall, my legs useless because of the throwing axe buried deep in my spine. Ice washes through my lower back.

The swordsman grins and advances. "We'll wipe this City from the face of the earth," he says. I pull myself away until my back is against the soft fur of my Goddess. My hand presses into seeping cold gash in her side.

Now am I in you eternally.

The swordsman advances. "I thought I killed you before," he says with a bemused smile. "How many times does it take for you all to die?"

All I have left is the utility blade on my belt, and I can't move my legs. I can't fight. But I can die with a purpose. I snatch the blade free and he laughs, but his expression turns to confusion as I slash the length of my arm and press it to the gash in the Goddess's side.

"Crazy fanatics," he growls, and he plunges his sword through my chest and into the Goddess, mingling even more of my blood with hers.

I'm growing cold.

Behind me, I feel my Goddess begin to stir.

I open my eyes—both my eyes—and they burn like flames.

I'm not alone.

We roar as we get to our feet, razorwire snapping like threads, tearing spears from the healing wounds in our chest and pinning heretics to the ground with them, claws slicing through ribcages and splaying them open like butterflies on display.

I'm not alone.

Ooli is here. Vapar and Lida and other old mentors are here. Presences I know only as venerable saints from epic historical tales are here.

Vallizha is here—her presence floods through me and we embrace in joy, though in the consciousness of the Goddess it is wholly inadequate to think in concepts like me, her, us.

The Goddess is all. We are all—and we burn.

And we howl in vengeance as the heretics burn, too.

Daybreak in San Diablo

Erik Grove

Daybreak in San Diablo smells like napalm and I'm the match.

The objective is Colonel Malo. Tyrant. Drug lord. Dead man. He's in a heart of a heavily guarded compound surrounded by thirty-seven soldiers. Not nearly enough.

Weak point is the east gate. Two gunmen. I move in close to the first. Creep behind. Hand over his mouth. Knife in his back.

"Shhh," I say, help him fall down to the dirt.

Thirty-six.

I take his ammo. You can never have too much ammo.

Switch out for my pistol. It has a silencer. Headshot like a whisper and the second soldier drops.

Thirty-five.

Hotwire the gate controls and I'm inside. Cluster of men by the carpool. Four of them. Maybe it's time to get noisy. Switch out for a grenade.

I take a shot to the back and I'm almost down before I know where it's coming from. Spin in a circle. Second shot and I'm seeing red. I see the sniper. Too late. Third shot. Lights out.

☆

Daybreak in San Diablo smells like napalm and I'm the match.

Huh.

Deja vu.

Anyway.

The objective is Colonel Malo. Tyrant. Drug lord. Dead man.

Creep behind. Hand over his mouth. Knife in his back.

"Shhh," I say.

Thirty-six.

Headshot like a whisper.

Thirty-five.

Hotwire. Grenade.

Hold on.

There's a sniper up in the tower.

I run for cover before he gets me in his sights. Switch out for my machine gun. Fill him full of holes.

Thirty-four.

I charge the four by the motor pool. Tight bursts. Center mass. Ratta-tat-tat. Thirty. I take a few shots but shake them off. Just flesh wounds. When they're dead I take their ammo. You can never have too much ammo.

I breach the compound with a frag. Swap out for my shotgun. Run and gun. Boom. Chick-chick. Boom. Twenty-eight.

Down the hall. They're in the corners. They're coming out of doors. Boom. Chick-chick. Boom. Damn. Missed and I'm taking heavy fire. Crouch down. Seeing red. Wait it out. Catch my breath. Frag out.

Twenty-six.

Malo is close. I can feel it. This is almost over. Switch back to the machine gun. Reload.

"Malo, you bastard, you can't run from me!" I shout and I see one of his lackeys at the end of the hall. Lackey throws something and it lands with a *tink-tink*.

Oh shit. Frag.

Boom.

Daybreak in San Diablo. Again.

What the fuck?

Two soldiers by the east gate. I hide and watch them. They don't move. They don't even blink. Are they even breathing? Am I losing my mind?

I walk toward them. "Hi," I say. "Do you remember me? I feel like we've done this before."

They shoot me and I die.

I see my body. Linger over it like a ghost. It doesn't hurt. I'm not afraid. I feel nothing.

Daybreak in San Diablo which doesn't even make any sense. San means "saint" and "Diablo" means devil. Saint Devil? That's the name of a city? Who would name a city that?

And where are the people? There's no one here except Colonel Malo and his thirty-seven soldiers. I need answers. I need Malo.

Tyrant. Drug lord. Dead man.

Knife. Pistol with a silencer. Counter-snipe the sniper. Mow down the motor pool crew. Take their ammo. You can never have too much ammo.

Into the compound. Boom. Chick-chick. Boom. Frag. Switch out for my machine gun. Ratta-tat-tat. I take a few shots but I don't feel anything and if I crouch behind that metal crate in the hallway I'll be okay.

There's music here. It must come from speakers in the compound. I don't see any see any speakers.

They keep coming and I keep killing them. And crouching. I crouch behind that metal crate in the hallway and I'm okay. I walk over their bodies.

"Malo, you bastard, you can't run from me!"

I notice that all of the dead look the same. The same uniforms. The same faces. Why have I never noticed that before? I take their ammo.

I feel like there are too many halls. Aren't there too many halls? Just one hall after another hall. And what were the soldiers doing in all these rooms before I got here? Were they just standing in there with rifles, waiting?

Each question just leads to more questions. How did I even get here? Did I parachute? How do I get home? Why don't I have a radio or a cell phone or something? Why don't I have snacks? And what the fuck is in those metal crates?

The colonel is in a big empty room in the very center of the compound. No, it's not empty. There are metal crates. There are metal crates everywhere.

Suddenly, I can't move. Malo comes out onto a balcony. He shouts something at me in a language I don't understand.

Spanish I think. But I don't need to understand it. Because there are subtitles.

"At long last, Captain Bravo," the subtitles say. They are yellow and they float in front of Colonel Malo. "I have been expecting you."

And then doors open to my right and left and soldiers stream inside.

I look up at Malo. Something tells me that he's the key to all of this and—

Hold on.

My name is Captain *Bravo*? Seriously?

Malo produces a missile launcher from somewhere. It just appears on his shoulder. I'm in the crossfire. The metal crates are too far away. A missile launches. I wait for it. Maybe this is the only answer I'll ever get.

Daybreak in—*motherfucker!*

Okay.

Okay. Okay. Okay. Deep breath.

There's obviously something very weird happening here. I'm immortal. I must be a supernatural being or some kind of alien or something. Right? My name is Captain fucking *Bravo* and I'm pretty sure I either don't have a first name or my first name is just Captain. Normal people have first names. I think. I don't even know anymore.

It's not just me though. This city is weird. Where are the grocery stores? Restaurants? I guess it would make sense for civilians to not be out on the streets in the middle of a war but there should be businesses and houses and city things that aren't compounds. I guess this is a war? Am I the war?

I need answers. I need Malo.

Tyrant. Drug lord. Dead—

No. What?

Fuck Malo. I just need to talk to someone. His soldiers aren't an option. If past experience is any indication, they'll just shoot me. Past experience. Wow. That's weird, isn't it? They shot me and I remember it. Can't dwell on it. Need to move.

The compound is in front of me, so I turn around and go the other direction. The jungle, a green monster that surrounds me. Empty streets. Empty buildings. Inside there aren't people. There isn't even any furniture. Just some wooden boxes that break open like Easter eggs when I hit them with the butt of my rifle. There's ammo inside. I take it. You can never have too much ammo.

Search everywhere and there's nothing, no one. No photos on the wall. No dogs. Search everywhere and find myself back where I started. The compound is in front of me. There is nothing else. I have a knife. I have a pistol with a silencer, a machine gun, a shotgun. This is who I am.

I am Captain Bravo.

There is nothing else.

There is music here. There is always music.

Ratta-tat-tat. Boom. Chick-chick. Boom. Frag out.

They kill me in the hallway.

It's always daybreak.

I am the napalm.

I kill. I die. I am reborn.

The only darkness is between death and rebirth. That's the night.

I miss the moon.

Daybreak in San Diablo.

There's a rocket launcher in a wooden box in one of the empty buildings. I take it and I step right up against a wall. I fire the rocket at the concrete and die in the explosion. I do this seventeen times.

What kind of God makes a world like this?

I can't. I just can't anymore. Daybreak after daybreak after daybreak.

I drop my machine gun. I drop my shotgun and my knife and my grenades. I drop my ammo. I have so much ammo. I take off my clothes and I go into an empty building. I crouch. I'll stay here for forever. I'll grow old here.

The sun never moves. I am never hungry. I never sleep. I can't cry.

I never wanted to be a soldier. My father was in the army and his father. I didn't choose this. I'm so lonely.

The music gets faster after a while. It gets faster and I see numbers. They hang in the air. Like the subtitles. It's a count-down.

No.

Please no.

When the countdown reaches zero the music stops and it's daybreak in San Diablo.

I've been thinking about this war a lot. Colonel Malo and his men, when you really think about it, want the same thing I do. They want to be happy. They want to be successful, feel like they matter. They want to feel safe. They think the guns and the grenades and the compound will give them control over the uncontrollable. It's all just fear and loneliness.

And this war? I think we're just pawns. My superior officers, their superior officers, they give us all this ammo and what can we do but shoot at each other?

If I could just get them to listen to me, if I could share what I've learned, I know they'd see it too.

But they don't listen. They throw grenades at me. They shoot me. They kill me over and over again.

I forgive them for this.

Alright, this is seriously fucking tedious.

It's daybreak and if I have to just massacre everyone in San Diablo and crouch on top of them—up and down, up and down, like I'm bouncing my balls on their corpses—well, frag out, motherfuckers.

I run up and knife them in their faces. Shotty to the knees. Machine-gun-butt them until they're smears of red on the ground. I wait in hallways. I lurk behind metal crates with oblivion in my eyes. I rub their blood on my face.

I kill and I kill and I kill and I think of my father. I think about when I was in college and I wanted to take philosophy courses and he said soldiers don't need philosophy courses and I never took them.

Well fuck you dad, I don't fucking care about you. I am more of a soldier than you ever were. I am a one-man invasion. I am Captain Bravo. I am death.

Kill kill kill.

But he's waiting for me every time. Colonel Malo and his missile launcher on the balcony. I shoot at him. I throw frag grenades at him. I crouch behind the metal crates and I crouch over his dead soldiers and it's no use. The yellow subtitles mock me.

"At long last Captain Bravo. I have been expecting you."

I can't escape the missiles. I can't escape daybreak in San Diablo.

Daybreak in yadda yadda yadda. You know. We've been through this.

Have you ever seen that Bill Murray movie? The one where the day keeps repeating itself? The way he gets out of it is he learns the piano and he rescues a cat and he falls in love. Bill Murray escaped when he learned something about himself. Bill Murray escaped when he became a better man. I am trying. I am trying *so* hard.

But there are no pianos here. There are no cats. No women.

I see myself in the reflection of a metal crate. I'm not smiling. Do I ever smile? I try to smile. It looks like a scar with teeth. I want to be someone that smiles. I want to be happy. I want to let my hair grow past my ears and wear something that's not made of camouflage and canvas. Something softer. Something blue maybe to bring out the color in my eyes. I have nice eyes. I've been told I have nice eyes. I'd like to go back to Rockport. I'd like to paint the waves crashing.

I imagine myself smiling in the ocean breeze. I imagine myself in narrow red boat shoes. It's the first joy I've felt in so long. It's the first time I've felt like myself. Captain Bravo is a mask and the machine gun is a prop. I think I know what freedom is.

When they kill me I'm smiling.

Daybreak in San Diablo smells like pastels and the pre-dawn Atlantic air from my dreams.

The objective is Colonel Malo. A career soldier serving a regime at odds with US foreign interests. A capitalist demonized by racist and imperialist biases. He's no more wicked than the big pharma execs that bankroll the special interests that send soldiers like me. After all this time, I understand him. He's ruthless but who wouldn't be? His country has been torn apart in a proxy war. It's been bombed for election year politics and transformed into cartoonish villainy to assuage white midwestern guilt.

This—all of this—is wrong. I don't belong here. But I am a cog in a tremendous and terrible machine. My identity has been bludgeoned with shame and guilt and manipulated by the petty cruelty of the ignorant and hateful. There is a world beyond San Diablo and I must fight for it. That fight takes me to Malo. We are and always will be at odds because the world made us so.

I make my way through the compound with a clarity of purpose, a resolve, not just in my mind but in my spirit. It feels effortless, the knifing and the shotgunning. Frag out like the stream that flows around rocks, dissolving them to sand over millennia. Ratta-tat-tat like the wind that turns mountains to plains. This is the objective. This is where I must go. This is where I have always been. Daybreak.

I am a philosopher now. I am a loaded weapon of war. I am so many multitudes and conundrums and I am love and acceptance and I am grief and forgiveness. I have killed and I have been killed. I have faced the darkness before daybreak in San Diablo and I have swayed to the music, the ethereal sound that radiates from heaven and beyond from speakers I will never see or know.

And I have so much ammo. I always take their ammo. You can never have too much ammo.

"Malo, old friend," I say. "There is no more running. There is only now. I know you and I will remember you."

He appears on the balcony and his missile launcher appears and the doors open and the rest of his men appear. I shoot and I run and I frag out and knife and crouch. It is a beautiful ballet. It is a prayer.

God, are you there? God, I know you and I will remember you.

There are twelve left and then there are eleven and then there are ten.

"At long last Captain Bravo," he says.

Nine.

"I have been expecting you."

Eight.

But the missiles never do fire.

"At long last Captain Bravo. I have been expecting you."

Why doesn't he shoot the missiles?

Seven.

Maybe he's changed too. Maybe God has reached out to him as He has reached out to me. Maybe we are caterpillars dreaming of flight.

"We can stop them together, Malo!" I shout out and six and five. There are bodies, identical bodies, everywhere. "We can be free together!"

"At long last Captain Bravo," he says. "I have been expecting you."

Frag out.

Two left. Just one of them and Malo.

"At long last Captain Bravo. I have been expecting you."

He's in a loop. He's trapped in a glitch.

I kill his final soldier and we are alone.

"I know what I have to do but I don't want to do it," I tell Malo. I tell God.

"At long last Captain Bravo. I have been expecting you."

I didn't want it to end like this. He deserved better. We both did.

Switch out for my pistol. This is mercy, I tell myself. I take aim. Headshot.

"At long last Captain Bravo. I have been expecting you."

Headshot.

"At long last—"

Really? How many times do I shoot him in the head? Headshot. Headshot. Headshot.

"At long last Captain Bravo. I have been expecting you."

Oh come on. Headshot. Headshot. Frag out.

The music gets faster because of course it does. There is no way out of this. I am not Bill Murray.

"At long last Captain Bravo," he says and I shoot him in the face again because fuck it and he falls down.

The music changes.

Is that it? Are we done now?

God?

Father?

Nightfall in Gorodsky smells like rain and I'm the storm.

The objective is General Khishchnik. Despot. Terrorist. Dead man. He's beneath a nuclear missile silo surrounded by fifty-four Spetnaz. Not nearly enough.

Dust in the Machine
Wendy N. Wagner

A sentinel rose up from the depths of the terraforming station, its filmy wings vibrating as its segmented body snaked between walkways. Its CO_2 scrubbers hummed as it hovered beside Lana219. She couldn't help holding her breath. As much as she knew the security and cleaning device only saw her as an appropriately shaped heat signature, she still thrilled to watch it scan her with its red laser eyes. If she'd registered as anything other than human, it would burn her out of existence.

It turned away.

Lana219 saluted its silver back. "Nice work, Smaug." Only another Lana would have gotten the reference. Or Ashanti82, of course. She liked it when Lana219 recited fantasy novels. Books with dragons were a particular favorite, and as a Lana, 219 had thousands stored in her memory. Maybe she'd read one to Ashanti82 while they waited for her appointment.

"219, come in." The voice in her earpiece was all-too officious.

Lana219 just managed to hold back a sigh, and then was glad she hadn't set her comm unit to subvocal mode. Lana233 had only been elected division lead three months earlier, but Lana219 had already come to dread her voice on the comm. "I copy, 233."

"I need to see you in the engineering office as soon as possible." Lana219's earpiece gave a tiny burst of white noise, the sound of the machine stumbling to translate her supervisor's unvocalized tongue movements. Lana233 was looking for the right words. "I wouldn't want you to be late for Ashanti82's appointment."

Did everyone know Lana219's personal business? Her lips tightened. "I'll be right there."

She tucked the box of air filters under her arm, where they jabbed into her armpit, and trudged toward the elevator. Her boots clanked on the steel grating of the walkways. The smell of grilled tofu and cabbage rose up from a lower level, both appetizing and stomach-roiling. She should check the air filters on this side of the station.

A Maria nodded at her, headed for the bio lab. The Marias all looked happier these days. Oxygen levels were so good outside, they were prepping the first batch of human embryos for tank implantation. Not another batch of clones—real, actual humans. Ashanti82 was already dreaming about playing lullabies for the babies once they were born.

Lana219 jabbed the elevator button more fiercely than she intended. There was no guarantee Ashanti82 or any of the other Ashanti models would even be around next year. The elevator growled and grumbled as it brought itself down to Lana219's level, its doors lighting up but not opening. She resisted the urge to kick it. It wasn't its fault that certain clone lines, like some pieces of machinery, were failing. Nothing on the station had been designed to last as long as the mission had lasted. Seven hundred years was a hell of a long time.

The elevator doors gave a gasp of bad breath and stale farts as it opened. Lana219 slid inside. She had the space to herself, but it still felt claustrophobic. How many clones had ridden it up and down over the centuries? She could almost feel their presence, those other Lanas and Marias and Bolades, crowding over her shoulder and pressing around her. The toe of her boot tapped on the stained floor as the ancient thing moved down, level after grinding level. Sinead75, a tech expert who worked with Ashanti82, got on and shot 219 a pitying look.

With a strangled ding, the lift stopped. 219 pushed out while the doors were still wheezing open and made her way down the hall. The office door had been propped open, and Lana233 stood at one of the monitoring stations, her hands clasped behind her. She glanced over her shoulder.

"Thanks for clearing the debris around Surveillance Unit 79. It's nice to keep an eye on the front door." She smiled. It was a smaller and thinner smile than the one Lana219 made in photos.

"What do you need me for, 233?" Lana219 switched the package of air filters to her other armpit and resisted the habit to fold her own hands behind the small of her back. They weren't the same person, for Christ's sake.

"I wanted to ask you about the oxygen levels in Ova Room One. They haven't improved."

Lana219 gave the filters a pointed tap with a ragged nail. "I haven't been up there yet. I was just about to when you called me here."

"That's not what the system says." Lana233 tapped a screen with a fingernail. It was as unevenly chewed as 219's. "It logged your entry at eleven this morning."

"That's ridiculous. At eleven I was still in the stockrooms." Lana219 activated her wrist-unit and drew up the security log for the stockrooms. She held out her arm to show Lana233. "Look. Here's my sign-in. 11:02."

Lana233's lips tightened. "That's not possible."

"Sure, it's possible." Lana219 perched on the edge of the desk. "The system's gone buggy. It's old. Maybe it confused me for another Lana. A dirty barcode can be misread."

"Maybe. But the locks on the ova rooms run at the highest security clearance. DNA scans, barcode readers . . . maximum redundancy."

"The storerooms are like that, too." Lana219 glanced at the clock. "Run a system analytic, catch the bug, clean the barcode reader—it'll be fine. I've got to get to that appointment. I'll change the filters right afterward, okay?"

Lana233 had turned back to the monitor. "I suppose that's fine. The egg units aren't going to be damaged by a little dust in the air."

"Right." Lana219 hurried out the door, rolling her eyes behind 233's back. A bug in the security system. This place really was falling apart. And now she was going to be late.

She still had the stupid filters in her hand when she marched, full speed, to the infirmary. The little waiting area was empty. A hot wave of anger raced up her body. 233 had made her late.

"Lana219?"

Beside the door leading to the treatment rooms, a Carla model medical clone waved at her. Lana219 forced herself to take a deep breath. This wasn't the Carla's fault.

The Carla. As if she wasn't a woman, an individual. Lana219 tried to remember the physician's designation. She had a wavy black bob, and Lana219 was sure she'd talked to her at least a dozen times. Carla75? 95? Something that ended in a 5, she was sure. There weren't many of her model; making a medical officer's data core was an expensive process.

Lana219 dropped the package of air filters down on the nearest seat. "Doctor, I'm so sorry I'm late. Did Ashanti82 already go inside?"

The doctor's smile was gentle. "I'm sorry, Lana219. While she was waiting, Ashanti82 lost consciousness. We've admitted her to the facility, and we're running tests. We should have more information in a few hours."

Lana219's legs turned to pudding. She stumbled into the chair behind her and would have toppled over if the doctor hadn't steered her into its seat. 219 opened her mouth, but found the words trapped behind an enormous lump in her throat. Some dim, cyborg part of her brain began whispering Dylan Thomas poems.

"It's her data core, isn't it?" she managed to whisper.

"It will be all right," the doctor assured her, patting 219's knee. On the back of the doctor's hand, the faintly white lines of a barcode stood out. Under a black light, they'd glow a cool blue, but Lana219 could still read them well enough. 95. Carla95. Carla the liar.

Once the brain stopped integrating with a clone's data core, it was the beginning of the end. Somewhere in the lower levels of the base, a Maria and a Heidi were probably already activating 82's replacement.

After a long hour, Lana219 finally left the waiting area to check in with one of the administrators, a Yuki with wastefully long hair. The woman laid a warm hand on 219's with a Yuki's programmed gentleness, and in perfectly modulated tones suggested 219 return in the evening. 219 shook off the solicitous touch. She didn't quite stomp as she headed out of the clinic, and then froze when she saw 233 sitting in the waiting room, the box of air filters 219 had left behind balanced on her knee. When she saw Lana219, she tucked it in her armpit the exact way 219 would have and got to her feet. Her blond hair lay in its usual smooth cap, a fringe of bangs framing her broad forehead.

"What are you doing here, 233?" 219 was keenly aware of her own tussled hair and the creases in her uniform.

Lana233 nipped at her thumbnail. "I'm off-duty, but I keep thinking about that security entry and the clogged air filter in Ova Room One."

"Why?" Lana219 started walking toward the mess hall. Fuck Ova Room One. She wanted coffee.

"I had a thought, so I checked up on it. Ran a few reports." She paused, forcing 219 to stop, too.

"What did you find?" She didn't want to care, but something about the younger Lana's discomfort suggested a mystery.

"Over the past three months, there have been four different orders for replacement air filters on that level."

Lana219 frowned at her. "Projected replacement rate is one

per level per *year*. With the sentinels and the stasis system working properly, there's just not that much dirt in the air."

"Exactly. I also checked the security logs for Ova Room One, starting over a year ago. Nothing, right? Just monthly maintenance, what you'd expect for a room full of lizard embryos. Not even a Renee going in and out of there. Then, three months ago, boom! Someone's gone inside that room at least twice a week." 233 put out a hand. Her grip on Lana219's arm was painfully tight. "I'm worried."

Despite the redundant safety protocols and all their training, 219 was worried, too. When the station had been constructed, every possible contingency had been planned for. The clones in their nine varieties could fix anything. But what if they'd overlooked something? She quashed the notion.

"We'll figure this out." She patted 233's hand. It was like touching her own. "It's probably just a bug. A ghost in the machine."

"A ghost," 233 agreed, but her lips came together, thin and tight. Lana219 didn't need a mirror to know she was making the same face.

Outside the door of Ova Room One, Lana219 swiped her hand under the barcode reader. The red light flashed on. The system thought to itself a second, then ejected a finger-tip probe. She twisted her finger in its tip, scraping off a few skin cells for DNA testing. A red light came on as the scanner chewed on the information. She couldn't help but think of 82, her cells right now being studied for signs of degradation.

Then a flash of green. The door swung open. 219 took a deep breath, shoving away the image of her love.

The automatic lights hesitated a second, then flickered on at their lowest setting. Her boots crunched as she stepped inside. She lifted her boot and stared at it.

"Dirt," she murmured. "Lights, maximum power."

The LEDs brightened. Lana219 set the filters on the counter and brushed her fingers over the stainless steel floor. She studied the yellowish powder. It looked like the stuff topside, the anemic soil the team had first sterilized and then spent centuries trying to make habitable for Earth micro-organisms.

"But how'd it get in here?" she mused. Everyone going in and out of the station had to pass through the airlock, where they were deep-cleaned. This much dirt could never get past the top level of the station—when the sentinels swept that area, they zapped any stray dust motes floating in the air. That's why there was nothing up there besides a few lockers and a recycling unit. No one shedding skin cells to make the sentinels work harder.

Her wrist-unit vibrated: a message. She tapped its screen and frowned as she read: *Did you find anything?*

"For fuck's sake, 233, I just got here." She made a quick response—*Still working on it*—and took a seat on the room's lone stool.

She rapped the air filter package on her knee. She might not have any answers for 233, but she could at least change the clogged filter. She dug in her tool belt for a screwdriver and her canister of sealant, then jumped to her feet and unscrewed the cover of the air vent overhead. She didn't even have to stretch; the original Lana had been a tall woman. The normal scents of the station wafted out the vent, a combination of old soy, laundry soap, and a hint of unbrushed teeth. She eased the old filter out of its site.

"What the hell?"

The thing was caked in dirt. It was as if someone had blown up a bag of soil inside the room and then tried to suck it all up the air vent. She set the filter cautiously on the stool and reached for the flashlight in her breast pocket. She clicked it on.

With a loud *whump*, a gust of warm air pushed out at her. Lana219 stumbled backward. She hit her head against the wall and scrambled to her feet, her heart racing.

There was another loud *whump* and then a second rush of air. This time she also heard the faint sound of laughter coming from overhead—the tinkling sound of an Ashanti model, followed by the low chuckle of a Heidi. She sagged with relief. She'd just heard the recycling unit on the level above. Someone must have come back from outside and thrown something in the recycler. She'd never realized the air system powered the trash chutes.

She wrinkled her nose. It itched, probably full of dust from the air vent. She swiped it with the back of her hand and then stopped. Dust. In the air vent. The air system moving the recycling.

Her wrist-unit buzzed an alert and she glanced at it, then felt the moisture go out of her mouth. It was Carla95, and it was the highest priority alert.

☆

Yuki42 offered 219 a cup of tea as she waited for the doctor, but Lana219 thrust it away. When Carla95 walked into the counseling area, 219 jumped to her feet.

"The data core?"

"We're going to remove it," Carla95 said. No preface. No platitudes. As straight as an engineer—as straight as a Lana.

"Can she survive that?"

Carla95 leaned against the wall, the skin beneath her brown eyes pouchy with exhaustion. "The tumor is unusually large," she said. "When the 80s were implanted, it was just after the false oxygen spike. That generation of Ashantis was . . ." She hesitated.

Comprehension hit 219. "They were sped up, weren't they? Some fucking Renee gave the order to get ready for human babies, and they rushed the nurse models."

95 pinched the bridge of her nose. "An oversimplification." She sighed. "But yes. If anyone had understood the nature of the genetic errors unique to the Ashanti line, no one would have rushed the process. They would have caught it. Error compounded upon error over the course of weeks of growth—it raised the odds of health problems exponentially."

Error compounded upon error. The same thing had happened with the shortcut in the air ducts, 219 realized, only written on a much longer and slower timeline.

"Would you like a sedative?" Yuki42 asked. "We have to keep her under until tomorrow's surgery, so you may as well get some rest."

219 tried not to glare at her and failed. "I'll just go home."

☆

"My wife starts surgery in half an hour," Lana219 snarled, throwing open the door of her quarters. "I deserve a personal day, God damn it."

Lana233 gasped for breath. "According to the security system, Lana77 is in Ova Room One right now."

"Who?"

"She died forty years ago."

"Shit." Lana219 grabbed her tool belt off its peg in the wall. "When did the door open?"

"Two minutes ago." Lana233 wiped sweat off her forehead. "I set up an alarm on the system. Ran here when I got it."

They raced for the lifts at the end of the hall. The elevator chugged up a few levels, then opened.

"This stupid thing only runs through the residential levels. Come on!"

They raced up the nearest flight of stairs, bursting out into the open space of the mezzanines. Lana219 peered over the walkway. Down below, a sentinel cruised over the top of the residential levels.

"Can you send up a sentinel?" she asked. "Have it monitor the room's exit?"

"Sentinels haven't noticed a thing," Lana233 snapped. "I've checked all their logs. There's just the usual people coming and going." She slapped the call button on the nearest lift.

"Keep it posted there on max function," 219 suggested. "It'll cook anything that even looks funny."

As Lana233 tapped keys on her wrist-unit, the lift crawled down the shaft to their level. 219 wished she hadn't left her own wrist-unit beside her bed. She felt trapped like this. The only thing she could do was stand here and wait for the lift to arrive.

She clasped her hands behind her back and stared up at the slow elevator. "I'm guessing you got my message about the connection between the recycling chutes and the air system?" A sentinel streaked past, its wings buzzing like a hummingbird's.

233 nodded. "I checked the blueprints, and that is *not* the original design. It was added near the end of construction as a way to save on personnel. No need to bring on sanitation staff beyond the engineering team."

"We *are* the maintenance crew," Lana219 murmured. "Every clone has the equivalent of two Ph.D.s packed in our data cores, but out here we're just janitors."

"That's not true, and you know it." The lift finally stopped in front of them, and Lana233 waved 219 in first. "Not entirely true," she corrected herself. "Someday we'll also be the teachers of a new humanity."

"Ah, yes," Lana219 growled. "Lana: now in English teacher mode."

233 tapped the *Close door* button repeatedly. 219 thought about grabbing her hand to stop the annoying clicking, but luckily the lift closed and began climbing upward, sparing her the exchange.

The doors opened and the two women darted out. Their boots clanged on the metal walkway as they cut across the open space of the cavern. Lana219 skidded to a stop beside the ova room's door. The sentinel 233 had ordered to monitor the area glared at her with its fire-colored eyes. Its CO_2 scrubbers whirred softly.

Lana219's hand froze on its way to the door's security panel. A tiny smear of yellow stood out beside the barcode reader. "Dirt. From topside."

"Shit." Lana233 checked her wrist-unit. "It says Lana77 hasn't left. What do you think that means?"

"I think it means we're haunted," 219 said, and unlocked the door.

For a moment, she was certain the room was empty. The dim glow of the LEDs showed only the egg unit's stainless steel panels and the small expanse of dirty floor: no Lana of any designation. Then the sentinel swept its red lights through the door, lighting up a sea of dust motes roiling over the ground.

"What the hell is that?" Lana233 asked. The door thudded closed behind her.

"Don't walk in it," Lana219 cautioned. "That's not just dust."

The dust motes contracted, congealing around a spot on the floor the size of a small crate. Its edges seethed and pulsed.

There was no air current to stir it.

"It's alive," Lana233 whispered. "It's alive and it's watching us."

"Do you think that's what the system thought was Lana77?" Lana219 did not take her eyes off the block of dust. "Like the system thinks it's a copy of her?"

"I've got to get a sample." Lana233 stepped forward, test tube in hand.

The dust threw itself upward, its top twisting into a narrow spiral. It slithered toward the air vent.

Lana219 launched herself forward. She couldn't let it get back into the ventilation system.

The dust twisted around her. She felt it go up her nose and stick to her lips, gritty and dry. Scared, she squeezed her eyelids tight, but it ground into her eyelashes. There was no way to close herself against the stuff.

She remembered the sealant inside her tool belt. Her fingers found the zippered pouch and she thrust her hand inside. How much dust had already gotten up the vent? How much could the air filters capture? She felt the cool metal canister and grabbed it.

She sprayed blindly, pressing the nozzle up into the air vent. The dust spun faster around her, scouring her skin. It roared and squealed as it battered her flesh. She could vaguely hear 233 shouting behind her, but 219 ignored her. She had to seal off this vent.

The noise battered her ears, rising in fury to a screech. Then a sudden silence.

Lana219 stumbled and caught herself on the stool.

"Where did it go?"

"I don't know," Lana233 gasped. "It just collapsed."

219 spun around. She could see the dust collecting itself, pushing at the seam around the door. The station's designers had planned for this room to seal to near airtightness, but time and the inexorable pull of gravity had tugged the steel out of alignment. Lana219 had never noticed the gap, only a sliver's width, between door and wall. But the dust had found it.

"We've got to seal the door!" She lunged at the door, squeezing the trigger of her sealant canister. A bulge began to form around the door frame as she sealed the dirt inside the spray-on material.

"It's something we missed," she said. "Something from the topside. Some tiny microbe that came in on dirty materials."

"How could that much dirt get in through the airlock?"

Lana219 shook her head. "If the systems always worked perfectly, maybe it couldn't. But we've been going up there for centuries, 233. A picogram a year, it would still add up. And most of the material probably didn't come from topside. We make our own dust and dirt down here. Molecules of food in the cooking areas, dead skin cells—" She broke off, staring at the other model. "Dead skin cells! Can you think how much DNA is floating around in the air? There's pieces of all of us in that dust!"

She threw open the door.

It was like stepping into hell. Red light clawed at her eyes. She had forgotten the sentinel.

The sentinels may have missed the dust before on their random patrols, but now this one was *assigned* to watch the door. It had noticed the dust sifting out through the door, had registered the change in the air levels—and its job was to burn the filth out of the air. The red beams brightened.

Heat seared Lana219's face. The pain drove out training, thought, cognition. She stood frozen, caught in the dragon's fire. For a horrible second, she thought her lungs would explode, and then a fist yanked her backward. She hit the ground rolling.

She curled into herself. Was this how Ashanti82 had felt when they'd radiated the tumors on her neck? Was this kind of pain anything like her headaches? There was no facing pain like this.

Something crackled, and a first aid kit dropped beside her cheek. Her first aid kit, taken from her tool belt. She felt the cool slickness of burn cream spritzing over her eyebrow. "Are you okay?"

She blinked up at Lana233. Her face hurt. She held up a hand. Red blisters ran across the knuckles. "Maybe?" She had to cough. "Did the sentinel get it?"

"I think so. We'll have to check the ventilation system and close off the recyclers to make sure, but I think mostly, it's gone. Glad I got a sample." She held up a tiny tube of dirt.

"Thank goodness."

"I just . . . what the hell was that, 219? It moved like it had a purpose. Like it wasn't just dust. And the computer thought it was one of us."

Lana219 sat up to against the door frame. "Wasn't it? I mean, it was part dirt, but it had our cells, too."

233 shook her head. "That's a creepy way to put it."

"But accurate. What I don't understand is how it kept that DNA from degrading. I mean, if Lana77 died forty years ago, then whatever DNA that thing sampled from her had to have been at *least* that old. It shouldn't have been passing ID tests."

"It's doing better than our own engineers," Lana233 said. "If we could tap that microbe's abilities, we could improve the entire cloning process."

"Yeah, but first things first," 219 cautioned her. "If that thing came from outside in the dirt, maybe our job's not as close to done as we thought it was."

"You're right! Do you think we need to hold off on defrosting settler embryos?"

"Shit. I don't know." Lana219 was suddenly too tired to think. Her eyebrows hurt. Her hands stung. Even her lungs hurt. "I don't know anything. Except that I need to go to the infirmary."

"I'm ordering you to." Lana233 eased 219 to her feet. "Some of the burns on your face look pretty serious."

Lana233 led her into the elevator and all the way to the infirmary level. It felt nice, letting someone take care of her. Being taken care of wasn't something Lanas were good at.

When they walked into the infirmary waiting room, they stood by the desk a moment, waiting to sign in with the latest Yuki on duty. Lana219 looked from face to face. A Maria studied her wrist unit, a squint suggesting she was headed for an eye exam. A Heidi had her hand wrapped in a stained bandage. A busy day, but she didn't mind the way. She was thinking about the dust and its talents for manipulating genes.

She looked at Lana233, unable to keep from grinning as her engineering brain spun with possibilities. And Lana233 grinned back at her as if she was getting excited about the same prospects.

"Lana219?"

219 turned to see Carla95 standing in the doorway to the treatment rooms. The doctor looked far happier than she had the night before.

"82's surgery went well," Carla95 said. "We were able to separate her tumor from her data core, and scans suggest her brain is functioning well within normal parameters. She should be waking up soon."

233 put her hand on Lana219's shoulder. "I'm so sorry I made you deal with this dust crisis today. You should have been here."

219 shook her head. "I would have been useless here, anyway. And this thing—maybe it can help. If not my 82, some other Ashanti."

"Spoken like a true Lana," 233 said.

"Spoken like myself," 219 corrected. "Whatever that means."

Three Cautionary Tales
Tanner, Adalyn, and Liliana Simon

Dramatis Personae:

LILIANA (11)   TANNER (9)
ADALYN (6)   MOM (Lacey)
DAD (Joel)   OMA (Kathy)
OPA (Harry)   AUNTIE JESSIE
UNCLE ROB

ACT 1: Three Needy Cats

SCENE: Interior, the Kwak family farm. It is late Christmas Day, well past THE CHILDREN's bedtime but THE ADULTS have all been enjoying margaritas this evening and haven't been watching the clock.

THE CHILDREN have eaten their body weight in candy while no one was looking.

AUNTIE JESSIE
Tell us a story about a cat, Tanner.

TANNER

Once upon a time there were three cats. An old cat, a young cat, and a middle-aged cat. One was named Popa—the old cat. One was named JoJo. And one was named Poma.

OPA

The young, beautiful cat was named Poma?

TANNER

No, Poma was the middle-aged cat.

TANNER laughs. OMA does not look impressed.

TANNER

Poma was skinny and very, very long. Like a hundred feet long. And Popa was really, really humungous.

OPA
(indicating his biceps)
You mean humungous here?

TANNER

No, in his belly. He was one hundred thousand feet wide. And then the young cat, JoJo, was a normal cat.

One day, Popa was sitting in his chair, but he was a little too big for his chair because he was one hundred thousand feet wide. So he had to make a new chair, but where would he get all the wood? He went into the forest to get some wood. And Poma needed to sew another blanket because her blanket was too small, so she went to a sewing place. And JoJo was taking a nap in his kitty bed.

When Popa found the perfect sized wood, he cut it and got a chair. But then his chair broke because he was too heavy.

                    OPA

What??

                    TANNER

He was about three hundred thousand pounds.

                    OMA

Because he ate too much candy at Christmas.

                    TANNER

And then Poma sewed the blanket and she was trying to take a nap but the blanket was too thin. So she had to make so many more blankets, but that would take her a thousand years.

And JoJo, he needed a new kitty bed, so he found a new kitty bed. And JoJo and everyone else lived happily ever after. The end.

    Blackout.

ACT 2: Hide and Seek

SCENE: Interior, Kwak family kitchen. DAD is making lemon drops and offering them to THE ADULTS.

AUNTIE JESSIE
Hey, Adalyn. Tell us a story about a cat.

ADALYN
There was a striped kitty and a black-and-white kitty, and the black-and-white kitty was named Roadie, and the striped kitty was named Creamy. They had to feed themselves, but they were in the forest and they couldn't find anything to eat, so they were starving.

AUNTIE JESSIE
What happened?

ADALYN
They were wild cats. They ate an owl that had a mouse in its jaws. And then they were thirsty and they couldn't find a river, and then it was tomorrow. And then they found a river.

TANNER
Made out of lemon drops?

ADALYN ignores her brother.

ADALYN

And then they found a place to live.

AUNTIE JESSIE

What did the place look like?

ADALYN

Like a zoo? There was a zebra, a lion, a giraffe —

UNCLE ROB

My favorite.

ADALYN

— a seal, and a dolphin. [Beat] And an elephant.

DAD

You know what elephants are really good at?

ADALYN

What?

DAD

Hide and seek.

Blackout.

☆

ACT 3: Pulling Teeth

SCENE: Interior, Kwak family farm.

LILIANA, arms crossed, has watching the previous two acts unfold with mounting suspicion that she—like her younger siblings—will be asked to tell a story about a cat.

AUNTIE JESSIE
Hey Lily. Tell me a story about a cat?

LILIANA
Why?

AUNTIE JESSIE
It's for a secret project.

LILIANA
No.

AUNTIE JESSIE
You don't have to do it, I know goading you doesn't work. But Tanner and Adalyn told me one and I'd love to hear yours.

LILIANA
(speaks so rapidly as to be nearly unintelligible)
There's two little cats and they lived happily ever after.

AUNTIE JESSIE
Where did they live?

LILIANA
(suspiciously)
In a castle.

AUNTIE JESSIE
Where was the castle?

LILIANA
In Holland.

AUNTIE JESSIE
And what happened before they lived happily ever after?

LILIANA
They ate candy.

UNCLE ROB
What kind of candy?

LILIANA
ALL the candy.

MOM
I know what happened when you guys ate all the candy yesterday.

> DAD

You did not live happily ever after.

> UNCLE ROB
> *(trying to salvage the interview)*

What was their favorite candy?

> TANNER

Milky Ways.

LILIANA ignores her brother. She crosses her arms and raises an eyebrow, daring AUNTIE JESSIE to continue the interview.

> AUNTIE JESSIE

What's your favorite kind of candy, Lily?

> LILIANA
> *(handing back AUNTIE JESSIE'S phone, which has been recording these stories)*

The end.

Blackout.

GROVE

Erik Grove is a writer, long distance runner, and little dog wrangler doing things in Portland, OR. He enjoys tacos, robots, and using italics for emphasis. You can find his work in *Escape Pod*, *Buckman Journal*, prior volumes of *Space Cocaine*, and other esteemed places like his mom's refrigerator.

Follow him on Twitter @erikgrove for dog glamor shots, marathon training nonsense, and sundry writerly shenanigans or check out his webpage (www.erikgrove.com) for fun and prizes! *

*There is no fun. There are no prizes. There are otter photos sometimes.

KWAK

Jessie Kwak is a freelance writer and novelist living in Portland, Oregon. She writes sci-fi and fantasy with a liberal dose of explosions, gunfights, and dinner parties. She likes to make her readers laugh. She is the author of supernatural thriller *From Earth and Bone* and the *Durga System* series of gangster sci-fi stories.

You can learn more about her at www.jessiekwak.com, or follow her on Twitter (@jkwak) or Instagram (@kwakjessie).

McCOLLOUGH

Andrew McCollough writes science fiction, fantasy, and undecipherable scribbles. Mostly the latter. His work tends to describe unfortunate things happening to relatable protagonists and often involve magic or robots. He is the author of *Mermaid's Garden* and other short stories and his work is available at Grievous Angel and Amazon.

You can learn more about him at his website: www.andrewmccollough.com.

NAKAMURA

Remy Nakamura is a writer of dark and weird fiction. You can find his stories in *Escape Pod*, *Pseudopod*, and a number of anthologies. He is a graduate of the Clarion West Writers Workshop and currently serves on the Science Fiction & Fantasy Writers Association (SFWA) Board as a Director at Large. Remy grew up in Greece, Japan, and the San Francisco Bay Area. He lives in Portland, Oregon, where he spends as much time as possible getting cold, wet, and muddy.

RISTAU

Kate Ristau is the author of the middle grade series, *Clock-breakers*, and the young adult series, *Shadow Girl*. You can read her essays in *The New York Times* and *The Washington Post*. In her ideal world, magic and myth combine to create memorable stories with unforgettable characters. Until she finds that world, she'll live in a house in Oregon, where they found a sword behind the water heater and fairies in the backyard.

You can follow her online at KateRistau.com.

SHERRILL

Jeb R. Sherrill has an oddly disjointed background. Having stumbled through everything from performing stage magic and kinetic juggling on French television and in Las Vegas casinos, to teaching martial arts and circus techniques, to competitive sabre fencing, film and stage acting, dance, song-writing, and his ongoing stint as a popular YouTube person-ality, Jeb has the ADD of a 10 year old. Writing, however, has remained his greatest passion since early childhood, having also written a barrage of short stories and poetry.

Pinning down his style is difficult, however. His liquid, psychotropic images, philosophical undertones and pure unabashed strangeness have made fans across the Fantasy and Science Fiction spectrum. Best known for insane worlds, over the top characters and sometimes heady subject matter, his work may not be for the faint of heart, but reading it is always an adventure. He considers himself to be a fantasticst and a writer of fairy tales for adults.

SIMON

Liliana, Tanner, and Adalyn Simon are typical farm kids, which means they have vivid imaginations and a very normal, healthy curiosity about dead things. Adalyn adores unicorns and creepy crawly bugs, Tanner will crush you in *Starcraft* and *Settlers of Catan*, and Liliana will not be tricked into answering your highly suspicious questionnaires about her interests, thank you very much.

TEPPO

Mark Teppo divides his time between Portland and Sumner, and he tends to navigate by local bookstore positioning. He writes historical fiction, fantasy, speculative fiction, and horror, and has published more than a dozen novels. If he's writing a mystery, he's pretending to be Harry Bryant.

He also runs Underland Press, an independent publishing house.

You can learn more about him at www.markteppo.com, or follow him on Instagram (@mark.teppo). He's rarely on Twitter anymore.

WAGNER

Wendy N. Wagner's short stories, essays, and poems run the gamut from horror to environmental literature. Her longer work includes the gothic novella *The Secret Skin*, the horror novel *The Deer Kings*, the Locus bestselling SF eco-thriller An *Oath of Dogs*, and two novels for the Pathfinder role-playing game. She lives in Oregon with her very understanding family, two large cats, and a Muppet disguised as a dog.

You can find her on the web at winniewoohoo.com or on Twitter (@wnwagner).

More Stuff

Once upon a time, this project was called something else. It made us laugh. But there were some marketing issues with that name, and so we changed it. And then we thought about it a bit and changed it back, because that's the sort of second-guessing that happens when you're, you know . . .

Anyway, there's a mailing list. Sign up!

  http://spacecocaine.com

Sign up for future messages about Space Cocaine. We promise they'll be as weird as this reading experience has been.

Fancy Doodle Page

~~Space Cocaine 4~~, er, ~~Space Toucans 4~~—no, wait! It's actually *Space Cocaine 4*! Anyway, this issue premiered in 2022. We're not about to make a note about where and when, because it always turns out to be a lie before the ink even dries. Regardless, this page is where you can find the weird squiggles and doodly-bits that suggest you and the authors were in the same location once upon a time.